WILL GALLOWS

& THE WOLFER'S DEADLY MAGIC

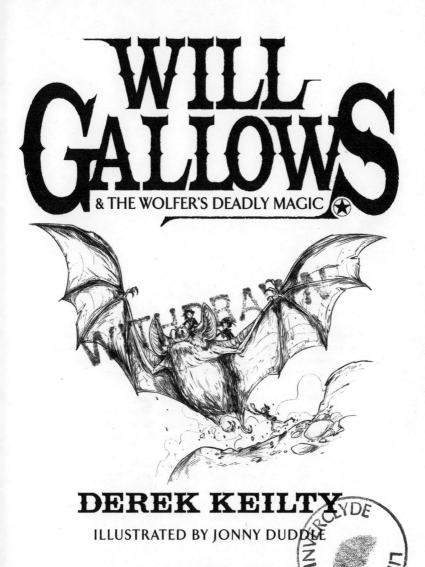

DEREK KEILTY

ILLUSTRATED BY JONNY DUDDLE

Andersen Press • London

First published in 2015 by
Andersen Press Limited
20 Vauxhall Bridge Road
London SW1V 2SA
www.andersenpress.co.uk

British Library Cataloguing in Publication Data available.

ISBN 978 1 78344 059 7

Printed and bound in Great Britain by Clays Limited,
Bungay, Suffolk, NR35 1ED

To my daughters,
Sarah-Jane & Rebekah,
with love

CHAPTER ONE

★

Blood-Red Ink

Stuffing a piece of fried bread in my mouth, I walked out the door of the mess hall in Fort Mordecai and almost ran into a breathless Captain Clint.

'There you are, Will,' he gasped. 'Been looking everywhere for you, the meeting's about to start.'

I swept my fringe up under my soldier's cap. 'But I was told it weren't starting till noon, sir.'

'Been brought forward 'cos everyone's arrived,' Clint explained. 'Mortimer's got a face like thunder – he's had to take the train all the way from Fort Westwood on the rock bottom for the second time in two days.'

I'd woken up expecting it to be a normal day's training with the sky cavalry. But my drill sergeant had

1

informed me the High Sheriff was calling a meeting of all the cavalry officers from the outlying forts of the Great West Rock and he wanted me to keep a written record. I was curious as the weekly meeting had taken place only yesterday and I wondered why the High Sheriff would call another one so soon. But I felt honoured to be chosen as note-taker too.

'What ya reckon the meeting's about?' I asked Clint.

'Your guess is as good as mine, must be something pretty important; High Sheriff wouldn't get us all together again for nothing.'

As we hurried across the parade ground, Clint commented, 'Hey, I hear this weekend's your passing out parade?'

'Yeah. I still can't believe it though. Seems like only yesterday I was packing my bags at Phoenix Rise and saying goodbye to Grandma. And now I am nearly a fully trained soldier.'

'How you been finding the training?'

'Be glad to get finished,' I replied. 'Ain't grumblin', training's important and taking notes is important, too, but I'm looking forward to getting stuck into some real sky cavalry stuff.'

Pressing an elbow to his stomach, Clint began to wriggle his forearm around, grinning. 'Y'mean like fighting snake-bellied trolls down tin mines.'

I laughed. 'Anything to get out of the fort walls for a while.'

Arriving at the High Sheriff's office, Clint knocked on the door and we both entered.

Inside, I glanced around the long wooden table at the seated sky cavalry officers. They acknowledged Clint and me with a nod.

The High Sheriff sat at the top of the table, his bushy eyebrows (white, like his hair) furrowed in a frown. He didn't look up. His eyes were fixed on an envelope he was clutching.

'Appreciate you coming to the meeting, gentlemen,' he said in a sombre tone.

I watched, growing more and more intrigued as the High Sheriff slowly removed an old yellowing piece of paper from the envelope.

'This note is the reason you're all here today – it arrived this morning with the fort mail. I'd like to read it to y'all.'

3

TO THE HIGH SHERIFF

At Noon Tomorrow On The Roof
Of Mid-Rock City Station You Will
Leave A Good Strong Windhorse With
A Saddle Bag Containing A Hundred
Gold Pieces. You Will Send One
Unarmed Soldier To Do This.
No Guns Or Funny Business.
I Will Be Watching.

If You Don't Meet My Demands
A Death Mace Will Explode On The
Midrock Like An Erupting Wasteland
Volcano. Innocents Will Die And
Their Blood Will Be On Your Hands.
You Have Been Warned.

An Old Enemy

The High Sheriff looked up. All the officers sat stone still, frozen expressions of disbelief on their faces. I felt a lump rise in my throat. The High Sheriff passed the note to Captain Clint.

Swallowing hard, Clint took it from him. '"Explode like a Wasteland volcano." But what could it mean?'

'Your guess is as good as mine, Captain Clint.'

'And what's a Death Mace when it's at home?'

The High Sheriff glanced at the file in front of him. 'Got no idea, and we got plenty of old enemies, so it ain't narrowed down all that much.'

'Could be a bluff,' said an older officer, Captain Grey. 'Some downbeat out to make an easy buck an' think we're dumb enough to buy it.'

'Could be,' the High Sheriff replied, 'though I gotta feeling it's for real.'

Captain Clint slid me the note and I stared at the scrawl in blood-red ink, as a chill snaked its way up my spine.

Out of the blue the High Sheriff asked, 'You're a half elf, Will – you ever heard elf folk mention a Death Mace?'

Although present at many meetings in the past,

5

I hadn't usually been asked to take part. I was only there to take notes. But I was pleased the High Sheriff thought I was worth including. 'Ain't ever heard of it, sir. I could ask my uncle Crazy Wolf just to make sure.'

'I'd appreciate that.' The High Sheriff cleared his throat. 'Obviously we ain't paying – the sky cavalry won't be held to ransom by anyone. I despise extortionists even more than bank robbers – we gotta bring him in. I've dealt with a few cases like this over the years but usually directed at rich folk, not the fort.'

'So we don't pay,' said Captain Grey. 'We catch him?'

'That's my thinking. He's told us where he's gonna be. We wait for him to collect the gold then bang! We take him out before he can be a danger or carry out his threat.'

Captain Mortimer from Fort Westwood shook his head. He was a string bean of a man with a big nose. 'Easier said than done. Especially if he's threatening to carry out some kind of attack on the rock. He's gonna have his eyes peeled for weapons. How do we bring him in?'

'Be willing to fly up there myself, though ain't so sure about the unarmed bit. But reckon I could bury a six shot deep inside my coat,' said Grey.

'What if he spots it?' Mortimer replied. 'No, too risky.'

'I'll go, sir,' I said.

All the officers stared at me. Then big-nose Mortimer laughed loudly.

Unruffled, I went on. 'An' I wouldn't need a six shot, sir, not while I got these.' I held out my palms. Big Nose laughed even louder.

'What are you planning to do, boy, slap him across the face while he puts a bullet in your gut?'

The High Sheriff smiled. 'Young Will here don't mean to slap him, Mortimer.' He shot me a wink. 'And for those of you don't know about our newest recruit's secret weapon, maybe he'll give you a little demonstration.'

Cupping my hands I concentrated hard. My hands began to burn and a wreath of smoke spiralled into view until with a *whoosh*, a globe of fire erupted from the skin to crackle angrily just above my palms. Clint, who sat next to me, drew back.

7

I stood up, propelling the fireball forward over Mortimer's head until it struck the office wall. It exploded into a hundred tiny fizzling flames but only scorched the wood – most of the fort, including the High Sheriff's office, was made from saddlewood, which doesn't burn.

'Well I'll be an ogre's toe!' Grey cried. 'Just what the heck are you teaching your trainees here at Fort Mordecai, Flynt?'

The High Sheriff smiled. 'I'm afraid I can't claim the credit for Will's aptitude, the boy's great-uncle Crazy Wolf is medicine mage down in Gung-Choux Village on the eastern arm.'

'I could see you have elf ancestry, lad, but I didn't realise you were practising magic,' Mortimer said.

'Thank you for offering, Will, but I ain't so sure it's a good idea,' said the High Sheriff. 'What kinda High Sheriff would I be if I let you walk into a situation like this when you ain't even outta your training yet?'

'Then *call* it training – field training!'

'The boy's itchin' for a mission harder than a sky cowboy with lice in his pants,' said Clint. 'And reckon if he's willing, it ain't such a half-baked idea on the face of it. Outlaw's gonna be looking for rifles, not fireballs.'

'I agree,' said Grey. 'Why, young Gallows's arrival at Fort Mordecai might just be a timely one. And like you say, Clint, this enemy's gonna have his eyes peeled for weapons or a trap … but the boy's different.'

He was right there. I was half elf, half human. My mother was elf and my pa was human and I was the first Halfling to ever join the sky cavalry.

Mortimer didn't look convinced. 'Hold on a minute.

With all due respect, High Sheriff, wouldn't we be sending a rookie in to do an experienced soldier's job?'

'Boy's more than capable, and has fought alongside us in the past,' said Clint. 'Got the courage of a rock lion.'

'So I can go?' I broke in.

The High Sheriff sighed. 'Look, I agree, Will, you probably got the best chance of getting close to this outlaw and maybe bringing him down, but I got a duty of care towards your safety. Now you're in the sky cavalry, you're my responsibility. We don't know what we're up against here.'

I didn't let up. 'But you know I can do it – you've seen me.'

'We could ride down and take a look at the scene near the station,' Clint suggested. 'And if you do put the boy on the roof, I'm pretty sure I could take up position as sharpshooter on the second floor of the saloon.'

The High Sheriff stroked his chin. 'You sure you'd be willin' to take something like this on, Will, when you hardly even set a soldier's boot through the door o' the fort here?'

'I joined the sky cavalry to make a difference, sir – why not let me start now?'

He paused, glancing at the note on the table then one bushy eyebrow crept up his forehead. 'Then far be it from me to get in the way of your field training.'

I sprang to my feet. 'You mean I can go?'

'We'll need to sort out the detail. You won't be alone. I'll arrange for cover – ain't gonna send you in there without backup.'

'I won't let you down, sir. An' if you're thinking about a good strong horse to fit the description on the note then you don't have to look any farther than Moonshine,' I said, volunteering my own noble and loyal horse.

'I wouldn't expect you to ride into this mission

on any other horse. I know Moonshine will do a fine job.' He rose slowly and folded the note back into the envelope. 'Gentlemen, if there's no other business, I'm wrapping things up. I want you to return to your forts and warn your troops to be vigilant over the coming days till this matter is resolved. And it goes without saying, I don't want a word of this breathed outside these office walls – Digger Scoops at the *Mid-Rock City Times* gets hold o' this, and there'll be pandemonium.'

★★★

I left the High Sheriff's office and walked across the parade ground, heading for the fort stable. The High Sheriff had said not to tell anybody, but it weren't like Moonshine was going to say anything.

The stable was located between the blacksmith's and the carpenter's shops and I went inside only to find Moonshine's stall was empty. Where could she have gone? No one else rode her, only me.

I heard a whicker and a horse's head appeared over the neighbouring stall. It was Koal, one of the other winged mares. 'I'd check the tack room, Will,' she informed me in a soft voice.

I stroked her nose. 'Hey, Koal. What's she doing in the tack room?'

'Been sneakin' in and out all day, won't say what she's doin'.'

Most folk on the rock don't hold with talking to animals. But elf folk have a bond with all animals. Critter chatter, as it's known on the rock, comes as naturally to me as soldiering.

I headed for the tack room. Rows of saddle racks and bridle pegs lined the length of the wall. And in the middle, Moonshine stood alongside one of the pegs, swishing her tail against her bridle.

'Hey, Shy, what ya doing?'

'Howdy, Will. I'm polishing the brass rosettes on my bridle, I wanna look my best at the passing out parade.'

I grinned. 'You're starting early – it's a whole week away.'

'My pa always said you should never leave stuff till the last minute. Oh, and since you're here...' She plucked a bristled brush from the wall and shoved it under my nose.

Taking the brush, I led her into the grooming stall and began brushing her beautiful white coat just above her wings. Moonshine is a winged windhorse, one of the finest breeds on the rock, bred for strength and agility. Grandma used to say that a windhorse can turn quicker in the air than any other breed of horse.

'Say, what happened at that meeting? Saw some anxious sky cavalry officers walking past my stable – ain't seen so many stripes since I last saw a stripy clattersnake!'

I chuckled then I glanced over my shoulder to make sure no one was about. 'Got some big news, Shy,' I said in a low voice. 'Been a note sent to the High Sheriff by an outlaw calling himself an "old enemy". He's threatening to destroy somewhere on the Midrock, killing innocent folk if the High Sheriff don't pay him a hundred gold pieces. And guess what – the High Sheriff is thinking 'bout letting me help bring him in.'

'I know you ain't kidding, on account your face is whiter than my coat.'

'Wish I was, Shy, but it's serious stuff. High Sheriff's put the whole of the West Rock on high alert.'

'What's he gonna do?'

'Well, obviously he don't plan on paying him a red cent. So we're gonna try and stop this outlaw before he goes and does something treacherous. The drop is at noon tomorrow – the outlaw is expecting a soldier to leave the gold on the roof of Mid-Rock station in saddle bags tied to a winged horse…'

'Wait a minute, why are you looking at me like that… You mean I might be the horse?'

'I sort of volunteered ya, Shy, hope you're OK with…'

'OK?' she broke in, ears pricking.

'I'm more than OK! Can't believe we're gonna be doin' real sky cavalry stuff instead of all this training.'

'That's my thinking, too, Shy. Anyways, I knew you'd be up for it.'

'But what are we gonna do?'

'For this one, Shy, you won't be riding down with Will Gallows, you'll be riding down with Roaring Dragon.'

Roaring Dragon was my elf brave name given to me by chief Red Feather of Gung-Choux Village. My Uncle Crazy Wolf was the village medicine mage and had taught me all there was to know about elf magic. For a long time my grandma, Yenene, had been dead against me learning elf magic on account of it having a dark side. When I was little she had even lied to me, trying to protect me, telling me I couldn't do elf magic because I was only half elf.

Once I'd started doing magic I thought for a while I'd become an elf mage like Uncle Crazy Wolf, but then a few months ago

suddenly I knew what I wanted to be.
It was like I was sitting in a dark
room when someone carried in a
saddlewood lamp. I wanted to
be a soldier and serve the whole
of the rock, not just the eastern
arm elves. I'd been training at
the fort ever since.

'Run that past me again, Will,' said Moonshine.
'You're going to be an elf brave again on this mission
and use your elf brave name?'

'Well we're certainly going to use a bit of elf
magic. That's what the High Sheriff says. We're gonna
hit the enemy with a fireball. The High Sheriff reckons
it's gonna take a little magic to bring in this outlaw. I
just gotta make sure I'm on target.'

'Y'always are, Roaring Dragon,' said Moonshine.
'Crazy Wolf taught you well. And if magic is needed for
this mission then there's no one better than you to do it.
The High Sheriff knows that.'

Since arriving at the fort, I'd been practising magic
whenever I got the chance. Sometimes the High Sheriff
would give me time off from my main duties to practise.

I guess he figured that one day it just might pay off. He'd seen how it had come in handy in the past. I was glad I might soon get the chance to show him that it had all been worthwhile.

Just then the drill sergeant's head appeared round the stable door. 'Gallows, you in there?'

I jumped, remembering I was listed for guard duty after the officer's meeting. 'Yessir. On my way to the north guard tower, sir.'

'Guard tower can wait till later,' he hollered. 'Your grandma's at the fort gate and by the look o' things, she's planning on moving in.'

CHAPTER TWO

★

City Slickers

I hurried to the fort gate to find my grandma, Yenene, yelling down the hill at someone. I almost didn't recognise her. Gone were the old ranch clothes and black shawl she'd wear back home at Phoenix Rise. Now she was smartly dressed in a long purple skirt, blouse and neat carriage jacket – city clothes. But what was she doing at the fort?

'Get a move on!' she shouted. 'Yer like an old man with them cases, grunting and puffing like a steam engine.'

'I *am* an old man,' came the reply. Uncle Crazy Wolf struggled up the hill after her, carrying two large suitcases. He too was dressed in city clothes: a brown suede vest and black greatcoat. 'And what have you

19

packed in here, bits of lead roof?'

'Grandma, Uncle Crazy Wolf, what are you both doing here?' I gasped.

'We've decided to make a week of it, Will,' Yenene announced proudly. 'Your great uncle and I are booked into the Mid-Rock City Hotel till your passing out parade.'

Crazy Wolf shunted up to the gate and dropped both suitcases, panting heavily. 'We were making plans for your passing out parade when it dawned on me that a holiday might be a nice idea. Your grandma's been working her fingers to the bone on that new ranch of hers and I thought it was high time for both of us to have a break.'

Yenene added, 'Then there's the fact you can't rely on the train service from the eastern arm, so we figured if we're already up here then we got no chance of missing your big day.'

'You're staying in Mid-Rock City?' I exclaimed. The note, the blood-red ink, an exploding volcano all flashed before my eyes.

'Will, ya OK? Ya look like you just seen a big ugly wraith!'

'Yeah, I'm fine, Grandma. It's just come as a shock, I mean both of you never usually stray too far off o' the eastern arm and especially not for a holiday.'

'Times change, Will,' said Uncle Crazy Wolf, 'and we've decided to ease up a bit on life. Neither of us is getting any younger.'

I wanted to tell them to go back, to take the next train home but I couldn't – the High Sheriff had given strict orders that no one was to be told about the threat note. I was a soldier now and I had to obey orders. If I didn't, I'd be booted out of the sky cavalry before I was even properly in it.

'We realise you're busy, Will, but we just wanted to let you know our plans. We don't expect you to show us around or anything. We're just gonna see the sights. Maybe take a trip to Edgewater and over to the old burned-out ruin of Phoenix Heights to show my brother where we used to live. And of course the highlight of it all – your passing out parade.'

'I look forward to seeing you on your big day, Will. Never been an elf in the sky cavalry before and we're both mighty proud.'

'Well, are we gonna stand here gassing or are ya

gonna help your uncle with these cases 'fore he passes out?'

I let the sentry know I was heading into town for a short while and then grabbed one of the cases.

As we walked, Yenene said, 'Still keep thinking you're gonna come down to breakfast. When you first left, reckon I musta hollered for you to get up a dozen times before it sunk in you'd gone. How are you getting on, son?'

'Good, Grandma. Training's going well and the High Sheriff's happy with my progress. How are things at Phoenix Rise?'

'Busy, but then show me a ranch that ain't.' She sighed. 'Funny how things change. I'd always hoped you'd stay on at the ranch and take over the reins after I go.'

I hated it when she talked like that. 'Where you going, Grandma?'

'You know what I mean. Can't live forever.'

Uncle Crazy Wolf grinned. 'Old Blue Feather who lives on the edge of the village is sure trying – he must be a hundred and twenty years old. Says drinking plenty of water and a good night's sleep is the key to a long life.'

'How's Moonshine taking to life here?' Yenene asked.

'Like a rock duck to water. We all know Shy's heart was inside Fort Mordecai long before her hooves, so it's like she's just glad to be home.'

Yenene laughed. 'Sure miss her round the ranch.'

'I have to say, Will, you look very smart in that uniform,' said Uncle Crazy Wolf.

'Thanks. I'm kinda getting used to it now. Sure is a change from rancher clothes and a sky cowboy hat.'

He grinned. 'I still think you need a little elf brave paint on your cheeks though – just to finish the look.'

'Don't worry, I'll never forget my roots. I've been practising my magic. The sheriff gives me time to do it. And hopefully I'll be able to use my skills in a cavalry mission one day,' I said. But I didn't tell them exactly how soon.

Yenene said wistfully, 'It's a pity your pa ain't alive to see the parade. He sure would've been proud of you especially since you've taken to it like a gutfish to Gung River.'

I smiled. Pa had been a deputy sheriff till he was treacherously murdered by his own boss, the crooked former sheriff of Oretown. It still made me real angry just thinking about it.

'Yeah, I'd sure have loved pa to see me at the parade.'

Pa loved his job at the sheriff's office in Oretown but he had a high regard for the sky cavalry and loved to see them ride into town or fly over our old ranch.

We were just passing the Mid-Rock City saloon when a whip-tail goblin spilled out through the spring-loaded doors and staggered into the sunlight.

'Well now looky what we have here,' he slurred. 'A coupla ol' relic slickers out spending their money. Well maybe you'd like to spend some of it on buying me a drink?'

He fumbled for his gun but Yenene had her rifle out and both barrels pointed at the drunk's face before he could figure out which side of his belt his holster was on, let alone grab his six shot.

'Yer ma never tell you appearances can be deceptive?' Yenene spat. 'These "ol' relics" just happen to be hardened ranchers, and these barrels are still smoking from a couple of rustlers I buried not two days ago.'

Uncle Crazy Wolf added with a scowl, 'Come now, sister, don't ya think you've killed enough for one week – got me worried you're gettin' a taste for it.'

I knew they were joking, but the whip-tail drank up every word like a shot glass full o' Boggart's Breath whiskey. A few passers-by crossed over to the other side of the road, worried a shoot-out was brewing. But the goblin threw his scrawny arms cloudwards.

'On second thoughts,' he drawled, 'maybe I've had me enough liquor for one day, ma'am.'

As we walked on, Uncle Crazy Wolf tutted. 'Well I thought as holiday-makers we'd have got a better welcome than that. Not sure the city's for me after all.'

Yenene grinned. 'Don't worry, once word spreads 'bout this little run-in, Mid-Rock City will know we kick butt.'

I laughed. 'Hope you two oldies ain't in town to stir up trouble.'

Yenene slapped my arm. 'Who you calling old?'

★★★

Mid-Rock City Hotel was a grand yellow building on a corner site in the middle of town. It had pillars, a first floor balcony and smart doormen at the entrance. A fancy purple sign with gold letters above the entrance said: *Mid-Rock City Hotel and Saloon.*

Once inside, Yenene and Uncle Crazy Wolf checked in. Yenene looked like a cat that had got the cream when the hotel manager announced he'd upgraded their room compliments of the hotel. 'Always happy to have family of sky cavalry soldiers stay at my hotel,' he said.

'Thanks for your help, Will,' Yenene smiled. 'You get back to the fort now, we'll be OK from here on and we'll look forward to seeing you in a few days.'

'Yes, we will see you soon, Will,' said Uncle Crazy Wolf.

I kinda wished I didn't know they were in town. I was worried about the threat. Now, on top of thinking about tomorrow and facing this outlaw, I'd be worrying about Grandma and Uncle Crazy Wolf. All the more reason why I had to confront this outlaw and nip the threat in the bud before he became a real danger to the rock.

★ ★ ★

I got back to the fort only to smell something tasty, like a nice beef stew, wafting from the direction of the kitchen. I suddenly realised I was hungry.

After lunch, I climbed the ladder to the guard tower to begin my lookout duty. Staring out over Mid-Rock City, my gaze fell on the hotel towering over the other buildings. I thought of Yenene and Crazy Wolf maybe busy unpacking for their holiday. I stared, too, at the train station at the bottom of the hill and particularly at the long slanted roof of the passenger terminal.

Tomorrow Moonshine and I would be alighting on that roof to face we didn't know who or what. What would this outlaw be? Snake-bellied troll? Whip-tail goblin? Would we make it back to the fort in one piece?

That night, when I crawled into bed in the fort dorm, I could hardly sleep for thinking about it all again. And when I did eventually drift off, I had a terrible nightmare where I was sitting up in bed reading the extortion note when the red ink began to run off the page, dripping on to the bed sheets until they were covered in blood.

CHAPTER THREE

★

The Death Mace

he next morning I went for breakfast.

In the mess hall, my good friend Jez – her black hair tucked neatly into her soldier's cap – carried over a tray with fried eggs on waffles and a mug of coffee, and sat down at my table. Jez was a prairie dwarf from the Wastelands and had been in the sky cavalry for six months. We had become friends a while back when she helped me track down the killer who murdered my pa. She'd been out of town yesterday with a few others to visit Fort Westwood, one of the rock bottom forts. I'd heard the visit had something to do with the new anti-slavery laws the High Sheriff had recently brought in. A lot of the folk of the rock bottom were dead against it still. I found it hard to believe that folk could think it was OK to keep slaves.

Jez smiled. 'Hey, Will.'

'Howdy, Jez. Hadn't figured you'd be back from the rock bottom yet.'

'Left at first light,' she explained. 'I wanted to stop in on Yenene at Phoenix Rise but there was no time.'

'If you had, you would've wasted a trip. She's gone.'

'Gone where?'

'Here.'

'Y'mean she's in Mid-Rock City?'

'Her and Uncle Crazy Wolf. Like a couple o' city slickers, too they were, dressed in fancy clothes and with a pile o' luggage – you'd have thought they were staying for a month instead of a week. They came early for the passing out parade – planning to make a bit of a holiday of it.'

'Where are they staying?'

'Mid-Rock City Hotel.'

'That's great they're in town – hopefully I'll see them before your big day.'

I sipped my coffee then asked Jez, 'So, how was your trip on the rock bottom – heard it were to do with slavery?'

'Long trip an' I'm not sure it was worth it.'

'What happened?'

'We had a tip-off about a mine boss called Titus Knott. Folks are convinced he's using slaves in his gem mine but he's assured Mortimer and his men that he pays all his workers a wage and we couldn't find anyone to testify against him.'

'Take it slavery was a big deal down on the rock bottom – ain't ever really been a problem up here.'

'Still is a big deal. Folks are saying it ain't gone away in spite of the new laws brought in by the High Sheriff. I saw a lot of it when I lived in the Wastelands. It was everywhere – in farming, mining, you name it. The slave masters would capture and force goblins and other folk to work for nothing – treated them real bad, too.'

'What did they do?'

'Put them in shackles and beat them if they thought they weren't working hard enough. I even heard of one slaver who used to *brand* his slaves.'

I gasped. 'Like ranch cattle! They sure did treat them like animals.'

We carried on eating. Suddenly Jez dropped her fork. 'Oh, I almost forgot. I brought you something from Rockfoot.'

From her pocket, she took out a pendant: a scorpion carved in iron on a leather cord.

'Practically grabbed it when I saw it,' she went on. 'I've been on the lookout for another for you since you gave me one.'

'Thanks. It's great. I love it, but you didn't have to, Jez.' I slipped it over my head. As it wasn't part of official uniform, I tucked it under my shirt.

'Say, what's this I heard about your going on a mission for the High Sheriff? Sounds exciting, anything you can tell me?'

'Ain't allowed.'

'Guess I'm snitchin' but couldn't help overhear some of the other trainees talking 'bout ya – sounds like some o' them ain't too pleased you got picked over them. I had to tell one o' them to shuddup, that they happened to be talking 'bout a friend o' mine.'

'What'd they say?'

'Won't name names, as hopefully that'll be the end of it. But one of them said he reckoned the High Sheriff can't see past your big elf ears to notice any o' the rest of them.' I wondered if I saw Jez stifle a grin. I smiled back. 'Must be something pretty important. Is it dangerous?'

'A bit. But I'll be fine.'

'Can I come?'

'Gotta do it alone, Jez. But be good to think you were around with that little bone-handled knife o' yours.'

She pulled it out of her belt. 'You wanna borrow it?'

'Can't, I gotta go unarmed.'

'Really? On a dangerous mission unarmed? Where ya going?'

'Can't tell ya.'

'Oh come on, Will, I'm telling you all my news but you ain't told me nothin'.'

'You're the fully fledged soldier, Jez, and you're pokin' me like a rancher with a cattle prod to break an order.'

'Bet you told Shy?'

'That's different.'

'Just wanted to see if I could offer some advice, that's all.'

'I don't need your advice, Jez. It's *my* business.' I hadn't meant it to come out like that. I'd meant to explain I didn't need her advice 'cos it was to do with elf magic. She looked a little hurt.

'So ya know it all, do ya? That what you're telling the other trainees? 'Cos if you, are then no wonder they're talking about you.'

'Course I ain't! Look, Jez, I didn't mean it like that.'
I wanted to tell her it was to do with elf magic but if I
told her that then she'd probably start poking me for
even more info.

Just then the drill sergeant yelled over at me.
'Gallows – report to the High Sheriff's office. Oh, and
I expect to see you this afternoon. Don't think doing
hotshot jobs for the High Sheriff gets you outta training
– still got a week till you pass out.'

A group of trainees followed the sergeant onto
the parade ground and I was sure I detected a look of
jealousy on some of their faces. I wondered which one
had a problem with my ears.

I walked past the post trader's store to the High
Sheriff's office. I knocked and entered. He stood at the
window, twiddling his moustache thoughtfully.

'Still OK about this, Will?' he asked.

'Yessir.'

'You *can* change your mind, y'know.'

'And let you down? I wouldn't do that, sir.'

'Good lad. Here's the plan, then. Captain Clint
is gonna be down there with ya, outta sight in the
saloon. Once on the roof, you'll wait with Moonshine

36

and the saddle bags, which will of course be empty, until this old enemy appears. Then you attempt to take him down with a fireball. The injury should at least disarm and confuse him long enough for us to close in for the arrest. Don't forget, Captain Clint will have the outlaw in his sights from the upstairs saloon window.'

'I understand, sir.'

'Got no reason to feel alone on that roof, Will, you can be assured. Clint is the best long-range sniper we've got in the sky cavalry and he'll have a long steady barrel covering the area the whole time.'

'Thank you, sir. That's reassuring.'

'You got all your equipment – the dried leaves?' the High Sheriff asked slightly awkwardly. He was more used to briefing soldiers on which rifles and six shots they should arm themselves with, not what kind of magic leaves they should bring.

I smiled, putting a hand to the little beaded pouch on my belt. 'Loaded and ready for action, sir.'

'Good. Now, I've suggested to your drill sergeant he give you the morning off training as I guess you'll want to spend time preparing for the mission?'

I nodded. 'I'd like to get some magic practice in and get Moonshine ready, too.'

'Of course. Well, take what time you need. I'll get the saddle bags ready and see you close to noon.'

★ ★ ★

The clock above the mercantile store seemed to drag as I tried filling the morning with fireball practice in a quiet part of the fort. My aim was pretty good and I managed to hit the bull's-eye more than a few times on the little target I'd carved on the fort wall.

Finally, as noon approached, I returned to the dorm. I felt my stomach churn. The wait was almost over.

The High Sheriff came into the dorm and informed me it was time to move out. Saddling Moonshine, we rode towards the fort gate. I saw Jez across the parade ground, standing outside the mercantile store. Lifting my hat, I waved it over at her, though I didn't expect her to acknowledge me after what I'd said about not needing her advice. Slowly she raised a hand, although it was half-hearted.

Once outside the gate, we took to the air, flying towards Mid-Rock City station which was situated at the bottom of the hill the fort had been built on.

'You ready for this, Shy?'

'Yeah, these bags of gold sure are weighing me down though,' she joked.

'We'll need to keep our wits about us, got no idea what kinda outlaw we're up against.'

'He's an outlaw who's about to learn he can't threaten the sky cavalry and get away with it.'

It was a short flight to the Mid-Rock City station. As we soared closer, the Mid-Rock City Flyer train steamed into the station platform like an enormous iron dragon, brakes squealing.

The engine pulled both passenger and freight carriages, plus horseboxes.

Moonshine said, 'I hate riding in the horsebox, it's so stuffy and there ain't even a window to look out of. Reckon they should invent a first-class horsebox for sky cavalry horses, what do you think, Will?'

'Reckon they should, Shy.' I smiled.

I glanced over at the city saloon across the road, wondering if I could spot sharpshooter Clint. I figured he was probably too far away to be of any use and that the High Sheriff had just wanted me to feel like I wasn't on my own.

'Hey, Will – you see that, Will?' said Moonshine as we swooped lower.

'What?'

'I'm sure I saw a big warty troll head gawking out the station office window.'

'Good observation, Shy, but don't worry, the High Sheriff has already cleared it with Hox Swillet, the troll railroad manager,

40

that there might be a soldier on his roof and not to make a fuss.'

I flew Moonshine down to alight on the Mid-Rock City station roof. Nerves gripped me like a tightening lasso as it suddenly hit me there was no going back. The mission to face the outlaw started here. I felt scared but quickly realised I couldn't let fear cloud my judgement. Instead I thought of stuff to help me: my mage studies with Uncle Crazy Wolf and all my sky cavalry training. I might need to call on all of it pretty soon.

I waited with Moonshine, trying to make it obvious that I was unarmed by standing with my arms out from my sides.

Suddenly, I saw a shadow move across the rooftop and then someone came towards me. My breathing quickened and I felt the cold sweat on my back.

The figure moved closer. And closer. Trembling, I struggled to piece together what I saw as my fear grew. A long cloak. A wide-brimmed black hat. Dark staring eyes. A face obscured behind dirty bandages. Hands clutching a six shot, bandaged, too. It couldn't be, could it?

'Imelda Hyde,' I breathed, scarcely even believing

the sound of my own voice as I whispered her name.

Shy had recognised her, too and whinnied. 'That filthy— But ain't she in jail?'

'Not now she ain't.'

I'd had a run-in with Imelda not too long ago when she'd helped the evil Gatlan brothers frame my uncle for murder and the destruction of a new fort on the eastern arm. The Gatlans had wanted to drive the elf folk off their rightful land so they could build bigger ranches and herd more cattle. I only just managed to stop them with the help of a brave thunder dragon called Thoryn. But here was Imelda again – back to cause more trouble.

Sticking out of the top of her backpack, I spotted a rifle. The barrel was tied with a rag to try to conceal it.

I saw more cold metal tucked in her quick-draw holster, a six shot blaster. Still a weapons freak, then. She spat out a gobbet of bacca weed.

'This ain't good, Shy,' I whispered. 'Ain't good at all. My cover's blown out the window. Imelda knows I can do elf magic. Of all the low-belly outlaws on the rock, it *had* to be Imelda Hyde.' Why hadn't I thought of her before? It made sense now. An old enemy with a weapon I'd never heard of before? She was the person who'd invented the stone spitter, for pity's sake. How dumb of me not to figure out she'd be behind this.

Approaching, her cold stare was fixed on the saddlebag draped over Moonshine's back. Then she looked up at me as she made loud animal-like sniffing noises.

'Well now, unless my nose deceives me, I'm pretty sure I smell me some fresh half-breed hide from way back.' She sucked in a gasp of air through her dirty face bandages. 'Only now it's gone an' got itself all clothed in a sky cavalry uniform. Will Gallows, eh? We meet again.'

Her voice, still muffled by the bandages covering her mouth, was rasping – like the hacking of a plague-racked miner or a prairie cat being sick. And as she drew closer, I felt bile rise in my guts at the stench from her clothes which smelt like rotting flesh. Imelda was a professional wolf hunter or wolfer, and by the smell of her, she must still be skinning those wolf pelts.

'Imelda Hyde! But ain't you still in Mid-Rock City jail?'

'Keep up, kid. Done my time – got out three months ago.'

She laid a bandaged hand on Moonshine's flank. 'See ya still got your fine windhorse with the nice plump wings I could carve me and sell,' she rasped. Her long dagger-sharp knife flashed in the sunlight.

Moonshine stirred, pawing the roof nervously.

'Easy, Shy, she ain't gonna hurt you.'

'Y'know I got a feeling the High Sheriff ain't treatin' the note I sent too serious, sendin' a kid to deliver my gold.' She peered at me sideways through the bandages. 'Unless his plan was for you to direct some o' that elf magic your old uncle bin teachin' ya at me.' She grinned. 'Wait a minute, I can tell by yer face I hit a nerve there, kid. That was it, weren't it, that was the plan?' And she laughed loudly.

I said nothing. It was time to act. I figured that Imelda guessing the plan didn't actually stop me from giving it a shot. Concentrating hard, my palms tingled as I began to conjure a fireball. Behind me, I heard a loud whistle – the Flyer getting ready to pull away.

44

Imelda flipped open one of the saddle bags and reached inside.

'Whaaaa! Where is it – where's the gold?' she shrieked, pulling out a handful of the straw the bags had been filled with. Moonshine whinnied, stirring nervously. Furious, Imelda checked the other bag before flinging it to the ground. She clenched her bandaged fists, eyes bulging.

'Cursed High Sheriff's makin' a big mistake double crossing me – he's got no idea who he's dealin' with or the power I wield.'

Explode like a Wasteland volcano. I thought about the note again, feeling my stomach churn. What had Imelda meant? 'What power?' I asked.

'You'll see,' she sneered. 'The whole rock will see! But by then it'll be too late!'

I had the fireball as good as conjured. I could see wisps of rising smoke twist past my gaze, feel the fire burst magically from my skin pores and cluster together.

Maybe you got no idea of the power I wield, I thought.

It should have been so easy to unleash the fireball at her and at such close range she'd have had no chance of avoiding it. But suddenly a strange powerlessness gripped me. Imelda had fixed me with a chilling glare that seemed to reach right inside my soul. My arms felt like a dead weight. My mind went numb. But what was happening? What magic was this? I fought to avert my gaze but like a rune snake during a snake poker game, Imelda had me in the vice grip of her sights and now she was angry – very angry.

'I'm sparin' your life,' she hissed. 'But only so you can tell the High Sheriff that if he's going to play games with Imelda Hyde then I'll always be one step ahead of him.'

She brought the butt of her gun across my face, sending me spinning backwards onto the roof. I only just managed to release the fireball before I fell. It showered me with fragments of fire, scorching my clothes.

Imelda leaped into the smoke belching from the funnel of the Flyer which had just started to pull away from the station. I realised she'd jumped onto a passing carriage.

Nursing my throbbing jaw, I heard shots ring out from the direction of the fort, the bullets ricocheting off the train. It must be Captain Clint from the upstairs window of the saloon. But he was too late and I knew he'd have no chance of getting a clear shot in all that steam, not to mention there was the chance of hitting an innocent passenger – the Flyer was full.

'Will, you OK?' Shy asked.

I spat out blood. 'Yeah, I'm OK.'

My head swam from the heavy blow. I struggled to pull myself up but collapsed back onto the roof.

'Wow, you're wobblier than a newborn foal.'

'I just gotta stop seeing two of you for a minute till I get on my feet.'

The Mid-Rock City Flyer sped outta town, steam spewing from its stack.

A Death Mace will explode on the Midrock like a Wasteland volcano. Innocents will die…

47

I thought about the note. A chill snaked its way up my spine. How was Imelda going to attack the Midrock?

Finally, I managed to get to my feet as Moonshine kneeled down on her forelegs to let me mount. 'What do we do?' she said.

'Let's get after her, Shy. Imelda's angry enough to do something crazy right now. There ain't a moment to lose.'

CHAPTER FOUR

★

Blades of Flame

I mounted Moonshine and we galloped off the station roof, Moonshine spreading her wings to soar into the sky, following the snaking rail track. Steam from the Flyer chased past us as I steered Moonshine upwards to avoid the choking sooty smoke.

'Tell me this is all just a dream, Shy, and any minute now I'm gonna wake up.'

'That low-down wolfer, Imelda Hyde, is a nightmare that's for sure – I'd forgotten just how much she gives me the creeps with those staring eyes and dirty bandages.'

'What's her game this time? I've a bad feeling her plans are a whole lot more sinister. Before she was sorta swept into mischief by the Gatlan brothers, whereas now I reckon she's got a taste for outlawin'.'

'I got a taste for planting two back hooves on her bandaged butt!'

We soared towards the side of the last carriage as the train rounded a curve, flying close by. Passengers gawked out the windows at us. A kid waved. Then I felt my blood run cold. Seated behind the kid, reading newspapers, I spotted Yenene and Uncle Crazy Wolf. What now? A day trip to one of the edge towns? It was bad enough they were in town, now they were on the train with a mad wolfer making threats to destroy the Midrock.

'Look! Is that her on the carriage roof?' Shy gasped.

Squinting through the steam I could make out the dark figure crouching at the far end of the last carriage. 'Yup. That's her. Can you get me over there, Shy?'

'No problem.'

Moonshine swooped over the top of the speeding carriages to alight a safe distance from Imelda. I dismounted. Imelda was still crouching at the far end, hunched over something. She hadn't even seen me landing. What was she doing? I moved closer.

50

Imelda wielded a long sceptre-like object in two hands.

'You're persistent, soldier. Either that or plain stupid,' she hooted.

It was the most fearsome piece of weaponry I'd ever set eyes on. An iron rod handle about an arm's length topped with a head-sized iron ball covered in dagger-sharp spikes, with two longer ones which stuck out like horns. Barbed twine snaked its way from the orb down the handle shaft, leaving a gap half-way down for Imelda's bandaged hand.

I stared at the orb. It seemed to glow. 'What is it?'

'You're the kid with the elf mage uncle, you should recognise magic when you see it. On second thoughts, maybe I'm being a bit harsh, ain't no way you seen magic like *this* before. No one has. And it'll be the last time you see it. I call it the Death Mace, the most powerful weapon on the West Rock – capable of blowing this whole train to smithereens.'

The orb began to glow more intensely. The vicious spikes sticking out of the mace head became deadly blades of flame shooting from all angles, licking the air like fiery yellow snake tongues. I wasn't sure if they would burn you or cut you like a knife.

Chillingly, the orb transformed into the shape of an eye, a black pupil gawking all around before fixing on me.

Hissing and spitting, the orb began expanding, a swirling mass of angry flame – it looked like it would soon burst apart, scattering its flame in a ferocious fireball.

'Gonna get bigger before it explodes!' Imelda spat. 'And if you touch it, it'll blow up instantly.'

I didn't like the feeling I got in my guts, like the dark welling up in me, clouding my judgement. This weapon used elf magic. No doubt about that. But it was clearly the dark side of magic. The side my grandmother had warned me against.

I was conscious, too, that Imelda was trying to make eye contact with me, to lure me in with her weird sort of hypnotic stare. But I wouldn't be so stupid twice and made sure to keep my gaze no higher than her bandaged mouth.

'The fool scum that is the High Sheriff will soon wish he had paid me!' Imelda seethed.

I had to do something before it exploded – but what? I was aware, too, of Yenene and Crazy Wolf directly under us in the carriage with all the other passengers.

I was still thinking when I realised Moonshine had taken to the air. With a loud whinny, she swooped low over Imelda, trying to land a hard hoof on her head. Cursing, Imelda swung the Death Mace, the heat of the flames forcing Moonshine to veer upwards into the sky.

Desperately, I focused my mind and shot a fireball at Imelda but she was too quick and in a lightning move she blocked it with the mace, the fiery orb swallowing up the magic.

I heard her laugh madly as she raised the Death Mace high above her head then smashed it down ferociously onto the carriage roof. The noise was deafening as the spiked head of the mace tore through the metal roof leaving a gaping hole. I could hear the passengers scream.

Through the hole I caught a glimpse of Grandma. She was herding the frightened passengers up the centre aisle to the door then over to the next carriage like they were cattle.

Imelda tossed the fuse-lit Death Mace into the carriage full of people then hissed, 'So long, Gallows.'

And she jumped off the carriage roof, her cloak billowing behind her.

I saw something, like a dark-winged shadow swoop alongside the carriage as she fell. At first I thought it looked like a black windhorse but the wing span was twice as wide as any horse I'd ever seen. But I had no time to wonder what it could be.

The Flyer streaked through some woodland, trees whizzing by in a blur of green. Scrabbling to my feet, I hurried over to the hole in the roof and peered into the carriage. The Death Mace had landed on the floor below and now spat out huge gobbets of fire. It looked very unstable, like it could blow at any moment.

Most of the passengers had got off the carriage but a familiar face stared up at me. Uncle Crazy Wolf. 'Will, what's going on? What are you doing up there?' he shouted.

'You and Grandma have gotta get outta there! That mace is gonna blow like a Wasteland volcano!'

'So much for our quiet shopping trip to Edgewater.' He motioned towards it. 'I'll throw it out the window.'

'No! Don't touch it! That will set it off. Imelda said.'

'Imelda! Y'mean this is Imelda Hyde's doing?'

'Yeah, she's gonna destroy the Flyer. Sent an extortion note to the High Sheriff demanding gold.'

'I can't believe it. I thought we'd seen the back o' that evil wolfer for good,' puffed Crazy Wolf.

I noticed the train was fast approaching town. Time was running out.

'I've got an idea, Uncle.'

'Who you talking to?' I heard Yenene yell.

'It's Will. He's up on the carriage roof. Says the train's going to explode.'

'Both of you get into the next carriage,' I called. 'I'm going to decouple this one with a thunderball.'

'Good plan, son. I'll help,' cried Crazy Wolf. 'But I'll need some leaves. My sister wouldn't let me bring any – said we were going on a holiday and I was to get away from all that.'

'I got plenty, now hurry and get off this carriage.'

The train chased closer to town. I thought of the

note: *Innocents will die and their blood will be on your hands.* Edgewater was a fast-growing city and many folk had settled there after the collapse of the western arm. It was now the second-largest city on the rock after Mid-Rock City. I daren't think what would happen if the mace exploded in the middle of the town.

Hurriedly, I clambered down the ladder on the side of the carriage and met Crazy Wolf and Yenene.

Taking some magic leaves from the little beaded pouch, I gave it to Crazy Wolf. Then I chanted the magic spell in the elf tongue.

'Wampan obe hokan kwikapawa!'

Gradually the thunderball, the most powerful spell in all elf magic, formed in my palms, cloud-like steam spinning furiously, whistling like a tornado. Uncle Crazy Wolf did the same and his thunderball soon swirled alongside my own, both growing bigger.

I glanced round to see we were approaching the edge of town – there wasn't a second to lose.

'Now!' I cried. Simultaneously thrusting out our hands, we directed our thunderballs at the coupling between the carriages. They struck, shattering the metal and freeing the carriage with the Death Mace inside.

It began to move away from the rest of the train, slowing as it did.

The Flyer sped on towards town, leaving behind the decoupled carriage, smoke billowing through the hole in its roof. Then, with an ear-splitting boom like thunder, the carriage exploded in a ball of angry yellow and orange fire. Fragments of the carriage walls, roof and undercarriage hurled far into the air. I stared in disbelief as a great cloud of dust rose up from the site and splinters of metal debris rained down. The explosion gouged out a huge crater in the ground, ripping up a long length of track. The Flyer wouldn't be returning to Mid-Rock City any time soon.

My heart pounded. A second later conjuring the thunderball, and I'd have been too late. I felt my stomach lurch. No one spoke. Grandma, Uncle Crazy Wolf and I stared at the devastation behind us caused by the Death Mace.

The Flyer slowed, pulling into Edgewater station. Passengers stumbled off the train to stare back at the destruction, dumbstruck. Townsfolk emptied out of shops and saloons and made their way to find out what was going on. A drunk staggered out of the station

 saloon holding a bottle of Boggart's Breath whiskey, took one look up at the smouldering wreckage then tossed away the bottle and staggered off.

'Where's Shy?' I cried.

A flurry of wing beats told me she was all right as she flew safely down to land nearby.

'You OK, Shy?'

'Yeah, though I'm kicking myself. I just couldn't get close enough with the flames. I tried to fly after her but her mount was just too fast and weren't like any windhorse I ever seen.'

'Spirits alive,' Yenene said. 'What the heck's goin' on? First day of our holiday and pandemonium breaks out.'

Crazy Wolf put a hand to his head. 'Imelda's back,' he muttered. 'That's what's going on.'

'She's back all right,' I said, staring at the plume of thick black smoke twisting into the sky. 'Back with a bang!'

CHAPTER FIVE

★

Wolf Tracks

'**H**ow in spirit's name has a weapon of this power and ferocity been invented, tested and, to cap it all, *used* right underneath our noses!' bellowed the High Sheriff. He was growing more and more agitated. He hadn't sat still the whole meeting but kept pacing up and down past the office window, his neck reddening the way it did whenever he got worked up.

''Cos she's done it before,' I said, 'with the stone spitters. Though I realise they ain't nearly as powerful as a Death Mace.'

We were back in Fort Mordecai: myself, Captain Clint and Jez who I had been asked to fetch and update on what had happened. Jez wanted to know why she'd been summoned but the High Sheriff hadn't told me.

61

After the explosion, we'd wasted the afternoon hunting fruitlessly for Imelda around Edgewater. Grandma and Uncle Crazy Wolf had been returned by stagecoach to the Mid-Rock City Hotel. I'd tried to persuade them to go home but Uncle Crazy Wolf was getting to be just as stubborn as his sister and insisted they weren't going to let a crazy wolfer ruin their holiday.

'Could this be a sorta vengeance by Imelda for us dragging her stone spitters to the fort here while she rotted in Mid-Rock City jail?' Jez mused, glancing at some of the fragments of the Death Mace we'd gathered from the scene of the blast. Stone spitters were Imelda's first invention: long cylindrical barrels of iron carved in the shape of a thunder dragon's head, fixed to a wooden base.

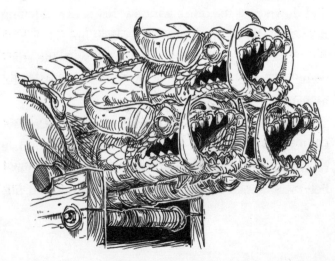

They fired rounded boulders
known as sky rocks with
devastating results.

'We had to take
away such weaponry
as a matter of security.'
The High Sheriff's brow glistened with beads of sweat.
'Furthermore she'd made them without licence and was
using them illegally to hunt and kill protected thunder
dragons.'

'Don't mean she gonna be happy 'bout us seizing
them,' said Clint. 'Maybe instead of locking her up we
shoulda hired her.'

'I wouldn't want that evil scoundrel anywhere near
my fort walls.'

'So she hates the sky cavalry for taking her precious
stone spitters,' I said. 'Hates them enough to start
dabbling in building more weaponry even more deadly
than a stone spitter.'

Clint frowned. 'If a weapon like the Death Mace
got into the wrong hands…'

'I say it's already in the wrong hands – bandaged
hands!' puffed the High Sheriff. 'And we gotta stop

her before innocents really do start dying.'

'How?' asked Clint.

'I'm mobilising several groups of soldiers. Some will scour the rock top and eastern arm, and check out the Hollow Hills – lightning has been known to strike twice in the one place.'

The Hollow Hills, near the edge of the eastern arm, was where Imelda used to live when I first came across her, and the place where she'd manufactured the stone spitters.

'Clint, you'll take Will and Jez with you to the Wynchester gun factory at the bottom of the West Rock.'

'Yessir.'

'Jez, you know the Wastelands like the back o' your hand, having been brought up there. And you've been down there a lot recently trying to make the slavers see sense. The Wynchester Demon Shot rifle combines magical and traditional weaponry and according to Imelda so does the Death Mace, so the Wynchester factory is a natural place to check out. You'll take some of the fragments of the Death Mace to let the factory owner examine them, see if he can tell us what sort of a weapon we're up against.'

She saluted. 'Yessir.'

'Will, so far you're the only one to have seen both Imelda and the Death Mace at close hand. Also your knowledge of elf magic, which is partly what this weapon is made of, will prove invaluable.'

I nodded. I felt proud the High Sheriff was tasking me with such an important mission.

'I am conscious, too, Will, that you're still on your training and so for this reason I'd like Jez to mentor you until you return to the fort. You will report to her and take any orders from her, too. Is that clear?'

I saw Jez try to stifle a grin as I mirrored my new mentor's salute. 'Yessir.'

I guess I was getting what was coming to me after my earlier comment that I didn't need her advice. Now I was gonna have to take not just her advice but her orders, too.

'Really, sir, I'll be fine. I wouldn't wanna hold Private Jez back.'

'Wouldn't be holding me back, sir,' said Jez.

'I got a duty to make sure you're properly trained, Will. Besides you couldn't get a better mentor than young Jez here.'

'Yessir.'

'Well then I think that's everything for now, folks,' said the High Sheriff. 'We're going after her. She's a former wolfer and used to following tracks but this time we're gonna track *her* down. Even if we have to scour the rock from top to bottom.'

So we made plans to leave first thing in the morning to fly to the rock bottom – Captain Clint, Jez and me – to check out the Wynchester factory.

★ ★ ★

After the meeting in the High Sheriff's office, I climbed the ladder to the lookout tower for my last guard duty before we left for the rock bottom. I was surprised when Jez climbed up to join me with two apples, handing me one. I guessed that meant she was OK after our sort-of fall out in the mess hall. Maybe she realised she could be a bit touchy over stuff – I was sure it was a dwarf trait but I couldn't tell her that or she really would blow up.

'You OK, Will? Sure been through it today.'

'I'm OK now, still can't believe it though.'

'Yeah. Me, too. Who'd afigured Imelda would have the whole rock on high alert?'

'Seems different, too. I know she's always been an evil critter but now there's something even darker about her. I'll never forget the way she held my gaze like a rune snake peering into my brain, taking control, freezing, almost paralysing. It was like her stare was so cold it froze me solid. I thought she'd forgotten a lot of elf magic but seems to me she's been brushing up on it a bit.'

Taking out her knife, Jez sliced off a piece of apple and ate it. 'Imelda used to be a mage, didn't she?'

'She was apprenticed under my uncle Crazy Wolf till she started dabbling in dark magic when his back was turned. She was cast out of the village for that. She tried to kill my uncle by setting fire to his tent but she ended up scarred for life – which is why she wears those bandages.'

'But didn't your uncle offer to heal her burns?'

'Yeah, but she was too stubborn. She left the village. Now she hates the elf folk 'cos she says they drove her outta the village when truth is she drove herself out by her wicked ways. Listen, about earlier, Jez…'

'Forget it. Ya got more to worry 'bout now. I shouldn't have badgered you to tell me stuff. Besides now ya *gotta* listen to me on account o' me being your mentor.' She grinned. 'Hope ya ain't gonna cause me any trouble?'

I grinned. 'Don't worry, Jez, you won't have to mentor me much.'

She pointed the knife at me. 'Careful. That almost sounds like the trainee-who-knows-it-all talking again.'

I sighed. We stared out as the sun began to set, leaving reddish pink scars across the darkening sky.

My eyes raked across the flat, dusty rock top. I said, 'I'm kinda looking forward to meeting the maker of the Wynchester Demon Shot and seeing where they're made.'

'Gonna be interesting to see whether he can tell us anything about Imelda.'

'What's it like at the rock bottom, Jez?'

'It's a mighty big place. Wastelands is just flat desert stretching to the horizon. West Woods is something though – green, dark woodland so thick that in some parts you'd think it were night-time. It takes your breath away. Whole place is dangerous, too. Critters that don't like climbing the rock live there and for some reason they're the nastiest critters ya could meet: underbears and Wasteland hyenas. And it ain't just the critters, it's the folk, too. They're just as bad, way they treat each other. You know slavery's still continuing on the rock bottom, despite the High Sheriff's ban.'

I nodded. 'Sounds pretty uncivilised.'

'Ya just summed up the rock bottom there in one word – uncivilised.'

'Looks like we'll all need to keep our wits about us.'

Finishing her apple, Jez sheathed her knife, patting the bone handle. 'I'm keeping more than just my wits 'bout me.'

Then she got to her feet. 'Reckon I'll turn in now, Will. Got us a big day tomorrow. It's a long flight to the bottom of the West Rock.

'Goodnight, Jez.'

'Goodnight.'

CHAPTER SIX

★

Where Demons Fear to Tread

The next morning I woke early. I could hardly sleep for thinking about Imelda and the trip to the rock bottom. I was a bit fearful but it was exciting, too, and better than normal training stuff – this was a real mission.

After a quick breakfast in the mess hall, we met up with Captain Clint and started out for the long flight down the rock. Flying was the only option as the train was out of service on account of the damage the explosion caused to the rail track.

Like me, Moonshine was excited to be venturing out of the fort again, especially 'cos we were going to the rock bottom – it would be the first time for both of us.

Although Jez had filled me in a bit about the rock bottom, it was no less impressive when a few hours later it finally came into view.

As we soared lower, she flew alongside me, crying: 'That big canopy of lush green treetops over there is the West Woods and that flat, barren land stretching to the horizon is the Wastelands where I grew up.'

Clint flew a buckskin windhorse up ahead of us and struggled to hold onto a paper map which was flapping furiously in the wind. 'Wastelands is where we're headed,' he yelled. 'I'm pretty sure the factory is somewhere near the bend in that river.'

Landing near a wide river, we rode towards the factory. I was conscious we were in the shadow of the Great West Rock, towering above us. Sure made me feel small, kinda like a dust ant crawling about the foot of an adult thunder dragon.

Situated on a marshy island, bordered by the River Ghoul, the Wynchester factory was a long black building with a central clock tower. At either end stood two tall chimney stacks like cattle horns, towering skyward like the Midrock, belching out clouds of thick dark smoke.

A sign above the arched entrance read:

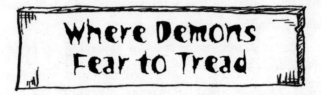

**Where Demons
Fear to Tread**

I felt Moonshine shudder under the saddle. 'Place is creepier than Mid-Rock City bone orchard.'

A stern-faced man with grey hair and pointy ears met us at the door, extending a hand.

'I'm Eli Wynchester. Welcome to my factory.'

'I'm Captain Clint and these are two of my soldiers, Private Jez and Private Gallows. Would you mind if we asked you a few questions?'

Eli nodded to us and I was sure I saw him take a second look at my ears below my soldier's cap.

Eli led us through a large room packed with dozens of factory workers – some wearing protective goggles – busily making weapons. The room was lined with rows of machinery, wooden benches topped with steam-driven gunsmith lathes. Pulley systems whirred noisily, powering the machinery, the pulley belts stretching up to the factory ceiling.

At the far end, we were shown into a small office with a messy desk, a few wooden chairs and some paintings of a very serious-looking white-haired man – who Eli explained was his late father and factory founder. He took a seat behind the desk and put his hands behind his head.

'So what can I do for you, gentlemen?'

Captain Clint removed his cap. 'We're investigating an extortionist called Imelda Hyde. You ever heard of her?'

He nodded, frowning. 'Sure I heard of her. Came to the factory a while back enquiring about work.'

Jez gasped. 'She was looking for a job here?'

'Yeah. I'll never forget the cheek of her, too. She said she'd be happy to start on the factory floor but that I'd soon be promoting her to the top job in design and planning. "Heck, I might even take your job," she crows, "and run the whole place for you." She was very arrogant.'

'That sounds like Imelda,' I said.

'What did you say?' Clint asked.

'Told her I weren't hiring. I read the papers and I knew she'd done a stretch in Mid-Rock City jailhouse –

74

I didn't want a crook working for me.'

'Done time all right, and not long enough if you ask me. Reckon the judge was too lenient,' said Clint. 'How'd she take it?'

'Didn't let up. Pulls out a bunch of papers – blueprints for the stone spitter, informs me it was her invention.' Eli looked at Clint. 'Says you stole them off her then threw her in jail when it shoulda been you in jail for theft.'

'That's crazy,' said Jez.

'I say I don't doubt her skills but that I ain't hiring. Times are tough. Why, only last month I had to let three of my workers go. Sales of the Demon Shot soared after the collapse of the western arm with the release of all them mine wraiths, but things have settled down a heck of a lot and there just ain't the same demand. And unlike some employers round here, I pay my workers.'

Eli was referring to the now banned slave trade on the rock and Clint nodded approvingly. 'You're honourable, Eli, just like I hear your pa was – that's the right way of things.' Then he added, 'But the factory makes other guns, too, not just the Demon Shot?'

'Yes, we make a load of different guns, but even sales of those are down.'

'So what happened with Imelda?'

'Then she shows her true colours. Turns nasty, shoves a long pointy-nailed finger at me saying I'll regret it, that she's got ideas. Big ideas. Says she invented the stone spitter and that she has ideas for other weapons even more amazing than the Demon Shot and a lot more powerful. Says she don't need me anyway – she'll go it alone. That she'd done it before and can do it again. Her eyes amid those dirty bandages were wild and staring. I figured she was aboard the next train to crazytown and wanted her outta my office.'

'She tell you about any of these ideas?' Jez asked.

'I didn't want to know. I knew I couldn't work with someone like that. If she was freaking *me* out, what would she do to my workers? She'd frighten them half to death.'

'Or stink them out,' I added. 'She smells pretty bad, huh?'

'Can't say I noticed.'

Captain Clint took out the fragments of the Death Mace from the train wreckage and placed them on Eli's table. 'She told you she could do it again? Well, she has.'

'What? You serious?'

'These are all that remains of Imelda's latest invention – she calls it a Death Mace. She ever mention it to you?'

He shook his head. 'What is it?'

'It's shaped like a spiked mace, the kind that ogres and wood goblins use, only there's a twist – this mace explodes with enough power to destroy a small town.'

Eli's mouth dropped open. 'Well I'll be— You ain't kidding either, are you?'

'Take it you heard 'bout the explosion on the Flyer?'

'That was Imelda?' Eli gasped. 'Wow! There ain't a weapon on the rock that can do that kinda damage. Cause that sort of carnage. Why'd she do it? You mentioned extortion, was that the reason?'

'Yeah, she wanted gold.'

'Why the low belly— Figures though. Once a crook, always a crook.'

Clint dropped his eyes to the fragments again. 'Do you recognise any of the materials?'

Eli poked through the pieces of metal, examining one or two up close. 'Gun metal, iron, like more traditional weapons. But there ain't enough for me to go on here to be more help.'

'Imelda told me she could merge magic with the mace, is that possible?' I said. Immediately I thought of the Demon Shot and although I've known since I was little it was a mix of traditional weaponry and magic I've never known how or in what way.

Eli frowned. 'Another merge weapon? I don't believe it, that's something I never thought I'd see. Course I have tried to invent other stuff myself over the years, Pa did too when he was alive, but we had no success.'

Clint asked, 'Can you tell us how the Wynchester Demon Shot rifle works? It might help figure out what we're dealing with here.'

Eli got up and walked over to a gun cabinet where he removed a Demon Shot rifle. He worked at the gun with a screwdriver, until half of it came away in his hand, exposing the insides.

As he did, some wisps of a pale smoky substance twisted up to the ceiling and I was sure I heard a faint groaning noise.

'Rifle's much like any other in terms of the basic shell and barrel. Where it's different is in here. See that little extra compartment there? That's what gives the Demon Shot its power.'

The brass-coloured compartment had elf rune marks etched all over it – symbols and letters.

'Don't recognise those runes,' I said.

'They're runes of the Wyn Chitaw tribe, my grandpa's old tribe. Each tribe got their own individual runes.'

'What's inside it?' Jez asked.

'Magic. I'll show you.'

Eli clicked it open to reveal small, coloured, glowing stones of different sizes. I could see that some of the bigger ones also had more rune symbols carved on them.

'The key with the Demon Shot is that it doesn't require the user to be skilled in elf magic,' Eli explained.

'Anyone can use it and that's what pa wanted.'

Demon Shot rifles had saved my life more

than a few times and it was great to finally find out what made them tick. I recalled the day when I'd last encountered a wraith – a fearsome horned ghost-like beast – in the stable of my grandma's ranch. I blasted it with a bolt of lightning-bright energy before it had to chance to suck out my soul and leave me like the walking dead.

I gasped, 'Those glowing stones – they gotta be full o' magic?'

'Right. The stones have a powerful spell cast over them, known only to the Wynchester family. Downside is the spell does eventually wear off and the gun won't work.'

'Runs outta bullets.' Clint smiled.

'Sort of.'

'So, getting back to Imelda… How could she make a weapon like this that harnessed the power of magic with the cold steel of conventional weaponry?'

'First, she'd need the materials and skill to put them together, which in her case may not present too much of a problem.'

'Then what?'

'A thorough knowledge of elf magic and its

applications to gunsmithing.'

'Well she's a half elf,' I said, 'and was trained in the ways of medicine magic by my uncle Crazy Wolf. But she'd forgotten it all last time I spoke to her about it – she wished she'd stuck at it.'

'Well she would need her memory jogged, perhaps through your uncle or at the very least through some magic books.'

'No way would Uncle Crazy Wolf help her – years ago she tried to kill him. And books on magic are hard to come by. It ain't like you can walk into Mid-Rock City library and check them out.'

'Say, you wouldn't happen to have such books at the factory, now, would ya?' Clint enquired.

'Of course.'

I met Clint's gaze, saw his look of concern and immediately knew what he was thinking.

'Where do you keep them?' I asked hurriedly.

'In the back office.'

'Can we see them?' Jez asked.

Eli strode through a door and we followed.

'Hardly refer to them any more on account I got all the magic spells and processes committed to memory.

My family has been making Demon Shots for over thirty years now though...' his voice trailed off as he stopped at a tall wooden bookcase.

'That's funny, I always keep them on that shelf, but they're missing.'

Clint asked, 'Would anyone in the factory have borrowed them?'

He shook his head. 'No one's even allowed in here.'

'Imelda,' I breathed.

'Was she in here that day?' asked Jez. 'Could she have taken them?'

Eli thought for a moment. 'The water.'

Clint frowned. 'Water?'

'She asked me for a glass of water. I left my office. It could only have been for a minute.'

'Reckon a minute's long enough to shove a couple o' books in your coat,' I said.

As we returned to the main office, I heard horses' hooves coming from outside the factory.

Eli glanced out the window. 'Looks like more o' your boys have showed up.'

I followed his gaze to see some sky cavalry horses approaching.

'If you'll pardon us, Eli, we best go check what's up. We're probably done here anyway. Thanks for your time.'

'No problem. You know where I am if I can do anything more.' He opened the office door. 'Oh, I'll have another look at those fragments; see if I can dig up anything.'

It was then I noticed it was not only soldiers who'd arrived, there were civilians, too: a well-dressed man and an old woman sharing his saddle.

I moved closer to the window as my jaw dropped – it was Grandma and Uncle Crazy Wolf.

CHAPTER SEVEN
★
Chief Big Belly

t the Wynchester factory entrance, Clint saluted the
cavalry captain. 'Mortimer, what's happened – you
find Imelda?'

'Not yet, Clint.' He nodded towards Yenene and
Uncle Crazy Wolf. 'Though might not be too long now
we got these good folks on board. This here's Crazy
Wolf and his sister Yenene – the High Sheriff sent them
down to me at Fort Westwood to hook up with yez and
join the mission.' He turned to me and smiled. 'Will, I
take it you don't need introductions.'

'No, sir.'

I helped Grandma off a chestnut brown windhorse,
muttering, 'You two are the last folks I expected to meet
on the edge of the Wastelands. And what's this about

84

joining the mission?'

'Got some big news about Imelda,' said Yenene.

She glanced over at Mortimer, who smiled. 'Go ahead ma'am. Ain't well up on elf magic so I'll let you two fill everybody in on your discovery.'

Crazy Wolf dismounted and took out a piece of jagged metal from his saddle pouch. 'This morning at first light, we went back to the wreckage of the Flyer carriage and had a look around and found a chunk of the exploded Death Mace. I examined it, hoping it might shed some light on the secret ingredient that makes the weapon so powerful when I was amazed to find dark magic rune marks of a remote elf tribe in the Wastelands – the Heng-Choke tribe.'

'Wow, an' we just been talking about runes in the factory, too,' I said. 'Though I've never heard of the Heng-Choke tribe.'

'You won't have. They keep themselves very much to themselves,' Crazy Wolf explained. 'They practise dark magic and from what I hear ... scalping!'

'Scalping? What's that?' I asked.

'Scalping is a barbaric act,' Crazy Wolf informed us. 'It was practised long ago by a few ancient elf tribes. When these braves killed an enemy, they would sometimes take their scalp. To do this the brave would shove their knee between the victim's shoulders, take a lock of hair in one hand, and with a sharp knife, separate the skin from the head, tearing off a piece with a loud cry known as the death cry.'

Jez made a screwed up face. 'Yuck! That's gross. What'd they do with them?'

'They would dry the scalp in the sun, comb it, then fasten it to end of a stick. They saw it as a symbol of bravery – a trophy. Sometimes a brave would have as many as ten scalps fastened to one stick.'

I grimaced. 'The folk of Heng-Choke sure are elves gone bad.'

'Sounds like just the sort of place where Imelda would probably hang out,' Clint said.

Yenene nodded. 'We went straight to Fort Mordecai and spoke with the High Sheriff who said it sounded like a strong lead and one that should be followed up without delay. So within the hour we were flying on windhorses down to Fort Westwood.'

I wondered why Grandma would fly all the way down then remembered the Mid-Rock City Flyer was still out of action on account of the explosion on the rail track.

Mortimer said, 'I know you're all probably saddle sore after travelling down from the rock top today but the High Sheriff wants this checked out as soon as possible. You reckon you could fly out to Heng-Choke Village and see what you can dig up?'

'No problem,' said Clint.

'The village is out beyond Oasis. The High Sheriff said you might know it, Jez.'

She nodded. 'I'm pretty sure I could find it.'

'Then afterwards you can report to Fort Westwood, rest your horses for the flight back up to Fort Mordecai.'

So we started out for Heng-Choke Village.

As we flew, I spoke to Uncle Crazy Wolf. 'I'm sure Imelda used some kinda mind magic on me yesterday on the roof of Mid-Rock City station. It was like a strange powerlessness gripped me, my arms felt like a dead weight and my mind went numb.'

'Snake eyes spell,' he said immediately. 'It's a dark magic spell used to confuse the victim then probe their mind like a rune snake.'

'Speaking of eyes, I'm sure I saw a grisly-looking eye staring out at me from the swirling flames of the Death Mace, you reckon that could be a clue as to what makes the Death Mace so powerful?'

'I don't know, could be. Maybe it has a secret ingredient.'

'Ingredients that all went up in smoke when it exploded.'

'Exactly.'

Following Jez, we flew for a while till a mist rolled in off the far west ocean, forcing us to land and proceed over the dusty ground. We rode for hours until finally we reached a small rise topped with thick tangleweed and clumps of trees. On the far side of the rise, a valley spread out below, the mist thin and patchy now.

Captain Clint threw up an arm for us to halt our horses. 'Wait, look there!' he cried.

At the foot of the slope, like some dark mirage, I saw a cluster of black tepees and two tall, black totems – the tops of which were shaped like wraiths' heads with curling horns. I felt the hairs on my neck tingle and an icy chill run up my spine. There were no bright colourful shapes or animal drawings like the tepees of Gung-Choux Village here.

'Heng-Choke Village?' I breathed.

Clint nodded. 'Has to be.'

'I guess we gotta check this place out, huh?' asked Moonshine.

'Not scared are ya, Shy?'

'Me? Are ya kidding? It just don't look like the friendliest o' places an' I'm only days away from becoming a fully-fledged cavalry horse like my pa. I really wanna make it to my passing out parade.'

'Quit worrying, you'll make it, Shy. We both will. Besides, we ain't even got there yet.'

'We'll tie the horses here and proceed down the valley on foot,' Clint instructed.

Shy breathed a sigh of relief. 'Great idea,' she said to me. 'Probably best if me and the other horses look after things up here. Watch your backs and all that – make sure nobody follows you into the village.'

Dismounting, I smiled, stroking her nose. 'You'll do a fine job, Shy.'

Carefully, we made our way down the grassy slope on foot and soon I began to pick out a few signs of life in the village: black horses, a smoking fire. We used tall clumps of tangleweed for cover until, at the foot of the slope close to the village, we hid behind a clump of rock.

Peering out from behind the rock, I noticed a rope tied between two trees near the edge of the village with what looked like a dozen horse's tails tied at regular intervals, casting shadows over the ground.

'What have they tied to those trees?' I asked, pointing.

Crazy Wolf frowned. 'I fear they are what we spoke of earlier – they are the scalps of the tribe's enemies!'

I swallowed a watermelon-sized lump in my throat, feeling my heart trying to club its way out of my ribcage.

Then, almost in time with my thudding heart, I heard the sound of beating drums. I was familiar with the elf drums of Gung-Choux Village but these were different, like a dull resounding plunk, soon accompanied by yelling and howling.

'Water drums,' Crazy Wolf breathed.

'Never heard of water drums,' I said.

'Made by the filling of the drum chamber with a small amount of water to create a unique sound.'

Jez pointed. 'Look, there are elf braves coming from that black tepee.'

The braves wore leggings and moccasins of a dark red colour, a few black head feathers, and a lot of red-and-white paint. Howling even louder, they formed a circle around what looked like a pottery jar and began to chant. Then to my horror, I watched one brave step forward, open the jar and take out a live clattersnake. He placed the tail of the snake in his mouth, gripping it round the thickest part of its body, while another brave stepped inside the circle, waving a feather wand to hold the snake's attention. Then the braves began to dance around in a circle.

'What are they doing?' Jez asked.

'It's a tribal dance, but it is one I'm not familiar with,' said Crazy Wolf. 'There are dances to the Great Spirit for good weather, for growing and harvesting crops. Though this one looks more sinister.'

As we watched, I saw something that made my heart pound even harder. What I'd mistaken to be a tall totem pole on the edge of the village suddenly jerked forward. It was alive – a horn-headed monster with staring eyes like two red-hot branding irons and a gaping mouth crammed full of dagger-sharp teeth. It moved towards us, eyes growing bigger, whole body growing taller like it was expanding. It was some kind of giant demon, arms stretching out with great clawed hands. Pa had told me stories of all the critters and creatures on the West Rock but I'm pretty sure he never mentioned a creature like this.

'Muuuuuwwaaaaar!' it roared, trembling with rage.

My heart pounded.

'Spirits alive! What the heck is that?' Yenene gasped.

'It's huge, whatever it is and I think it's spotted us,' said Clint raising his rifle.

'Twice the size of a dust ogre,' Jez added.

As it moved towards our hiding place behind the rocks, I saw that its neck was decorated with a gruesome necklace of animal skulls.

Clint fired three rounds which did little but make the creature roar even louder.

'Will, you or your uncle got any elf magic that could take this thing down?' Clint yelled.

The dark monster lurched forward, eyes staring, face frozen in a deadly fearsome scowl of dagger-sharp teeth. Its expression gave me an idea.

'Maybe. I'll try a new spell – try and freeze the critter in its tracks.' I looked at Uncle Crazy Wolf. 'It's one I been practising back at the fort.'

Focusing my mind, I blew on my hands. In seconds a white frost-cold powder began to coat my palms – powder that quickly thickened into a swirling dust. I directed the magic away from me, shooting a white jet from my finger tips towards the monster. The stream of powerful energy struck the head of the creature and froze it solid. But I wasn't finished. Lowering my hands, I directed the shimmering lightning-bright beam down its body until it too began to freeze.

The creature's roaring ceased as it teetered then wobbled and…

CRASH!

'Ya got him! Ya got him good, Will!' Jez hollered.

'Reckon that's way cooler than a fireball.'

Crazy Wolf grinned. 'Gave me *chills* just watching.'

'Wait, look! Someone's crawling around the creature's feet. They're bare-chested, like an elf brave.'

94

Edging closer, I saw that the totem-sized monster was in fact an enormous hollow shell, like a huge puppet. The creature was nothing more than a long pole draped in painted black skins, similar to those used in a tepee; skins that were now frozen solid. The figure that had been inside supporting the pole crawled for a bit then collapsed face down on the ground.

Realising the drums had stopped and the dancing elves were now looking over, I felt my heart race. But still I moved forward for a closer look at the brave who had been inside the monster. I crouched, rolling him over onto his back and found myself staring at an old elf, his half-frozen cheeks daubed in war paint.

'N … n … not welcome! Not welcome. G … go back!' the old elf stuttered, his body shivering.

'We mean you no harm. We're elves,' I explained. 'Mostly that is, this is Captain Clint and Jez here's a prairie dwarf.'

The elf squinted at us. 'Y … you elves!'

I guess we didn't exactly look like elves what with Crazy Wolf and Yenene both dressed in city clothes and me in a cavalry uniform.

'We wish to speak with your chief,' demanded Clint.

'S ... s ... speak with chief.'

'How long does the spell take to wear off?' I asked Uncle Crazy Wolf.

'Freeze spell? Not long, and he didn't take the full force of it.'

The frozen elf slapped his fat stomach with both hands like he was beating a war drum. 'M ... me Chief Big Belly, me Chief Big Belly,' he cried.

'Uh-oh, I think we got trouble,' warned Jez.

I looked up only to see the dancing braves and others were now running towards us from the village, their spears held high.

'Spirits alive!' I cried. 'Now why didn't I bring my face paint?'

Soon, they clustered round us, thrusting their spears.

'I've got a bad feeling about this,' said Clint.

Yenene rolled her eyes. 'And just when we were getting along so well with Big Belly here.'

'You harm Chief. You die!' the taller of the braves rasped.

'We harm no one,' Yenene snapped. 'Can't you see we're trying to help him. He's hurt his head. Now quit pokin' them spears an' help us get him some water.'

97

The biggest brave stared at her, lips puckered and frowning. She stared back at him. 'Well?'

He elbowed the brave beside him who kneeled to give Yenene a water container which she put to the chief's lips. He drank. Then she poured it over his face and the chief spluttered and coughed. The spears jabbed closer.

'Keep your hair on, I'm trying to thaw him out.'

I cringed. If there was a list of wrong things to say to a bunch of elf scalpers standing right beside a tree full of hanging scalps, then that would be top.

'Why you come to my village?'

'I am Crazy Wolf, medicine mage of Gung-Choux Village.'

The elf braves looked him up and down, frowning.

'We need your help,' said Yenene. 'We seek pow wow with you. We promise we won't take up too much of your time then we'll be outta your—'

'We'll leave,' I broke in before Grandma made another hair pun. Nearby the shadows of bobbing scalps cast long shadows on the ground where the chief lay.

The tallest brave spat, 'Heng-Choke no pow wow!'

But the chief's hand shot out and grabbed Yenene by the wrist. 'Wait. Big Belly pow wow with this one.' And he grinned a broken-toothed grin.

'Why we trust them?' the brave protested.

'These folk elves like us.'

Yenene smiled back. 'That's the spirit. Now ya got any coffee, been a heck of a long ride to get out here. By the way, why'd you have to live smack in the middle of the Wastelands anyway?'

In half an hour we were seated around a roaring camp fire with an iron pot of bubbling water over the flames.

Behind us, Chief Big Belly's black tepee towered into the sky. Chief Big Belly was small and skinny but his belly was as big as a drum. He was bald and sat with his legs crossed and head adorned with a tribal black feather headdress.

He grinned, motioning a hand towards the now thawing puppet creature. 'Monster enough to scare most folk but not you.' He looked at me. 'Magic strong in you, young one.'

'Got my uncle Crazy Wolf to thank for that. I was apprenticed under him for a while when I lived in Gung-Choux Village.'

'Stubbornness has won you pow wow with Chief Big Belly. How I help you?'

'We're looking for someone, a wolfer named Imelda Hyde,' I said. 'We think she might've been here. She is a half elf like me. Her face and body is wrapped in bandages. She wears a black cloak and a black, wide-brimmed hat. Oh, and she smells pretty bad. My grandma and great uncle found your tribe's rune marks on a weapon she has been using.'

He took a great gasp of air, like I'd stabbed him with Jez's little bone-handled knife. His expression darkened and when he spoke, his voice was tinged with venom.

'Imelda Hyde – I know not this name. But the cursed one you speak of lived among us for a time. She called herself *Black Raven*.'

'She lived here?' I gasped.

The other braves stirred uneasily. Some clenched fists and teeth. Seemed we'd hit a nerve.

Big Belly nodded slowly. 'Crawled in to our village like wolf. Lay down beneath our totem. At first we unsure about her. You have seen we Heng-Choke not welcoming of new folk.'

Yenene smiled. 'Over-cautious maybe. Heck, if I ranched in the Wastelands, I'd be the same.'

The chief smiled back. 'Black Raven wish to know ways of medicine mage; to learn from village medicine mage, Dancing Snake. She say her tribe cast her out for using dark magic. I tell her we embrace dark magic … because of Heng-Choke tragedy.'

'Tragedy?' said Clint. 'I don't understand.'

'Look around. You see no little ones. Our children taken from us, stolen away in night – by masked raiders over many years. Heart of village broken again and again. We paint totem black as sign of mourning then over time we hear Wasteland folk think we turn evil. They say we practise dark magic and scalping. At first we hurt at this. Then we decide it no bad thing. It maybe scare masked raiders from come back. Dark magic protect us.'

He must've seen me glance up at the blowing scalps, and added, 'Scalps not real – horse hair.'

'You think Imelda had something to do with the abduction of the children?'

'We no think so. Children taken long before Black Raven come. When she hear of our tragedy she say she learn quickly from Dancing Snake and that two mages better than one, protect us from raiders. We feel we cannot turn her away. We make big mistake.'

'Why, what happened?'

'Dancing Snake was my eldest daughter.' The chief began choking back a sob. Yenene offered him a handkerchief and he took it and blew his nose so loud it sounded like the fort bugle. 'At first, she and Black Raven not only mage and apprentice, but friends too. But more tragedy. One day, Dancing Snake take Black Raven to river to pick plants for medicine magic and never come back.'

'What happened?'

'We do not know. When missing for some time, we search by river – find remains of camp fire but no sign of them. We search all night. The next morning our fears confirmed. Dancing Snake's body washed up on river bank. We do not know what happened, but her skin covered in burns.'

'I'm sorry to hear that,' said Clint.

'Me too,' I added. 'Burns? What do you think happened?'

'They practised much magic together – maybe spell go wrong. Maybe Black Raven feel guilty and flee. Or maybe they have disagreement and she killed her. We do not know but we never see her again.'

'You've had your fair share of misery.' Yenene handed the chief another handkerchief.

He took Yenene's hand and squeezed it. 'You very understanding.'

'Why did you not report either of these tragedies to the sky cavalry?' Clint asked.

'We have no winged horses to fly us to cavalry fort. We feel, too, that cavalry care little for Heng-Choke and would be no help.'

Clint sighed. 'Shoulda let us decide whether we could help or not.'

Yenene wriggled her hand free and glanced at the sky. 'Gonna get dark soon. Maybe we oughta get going?'

Clint rose to his feet. 'Yeah, maybe we should, it's a long ride to Fort Westwood.'

'No. You spend night here,' the chief offered, smiling at Yenene. 'Plenty of room in Big Belly's tepee.'

'Thank you Chief, but I wouldn't dream of taking up your belly room,' Yenene replied. 'Besides, tepees make me claustrophobic – too long living in a ranch house.'

'You may not have much confidence in us but I would, with your permission, like to report your missing children to the High Sheriff,' Clint said.

The chief nodded. 'Chief Big Belly give permission.'

We left Heng-Choke Village, picking up the horses on the rise. It was agreed we would fly to Fort Westwood and spend the night there. The horses would need to be rested before the long flight back up to Fort Mordecai.

'So Imelda, or "Black Raven", shows up in a remote

elf village to hone her magic skills and while she's there an elf mage ends up dead. I think it's too much of a coincidence,' I said as we rode the dusty trail through the Wastelands.

'Trouble seems to follow Imelda like a bad smell,' said Jez.

'She *is* the bad smell,' I added.

Yenene frowned. 'A spell that went wrong – what kind of spells were they practising – a spell that leaves you covered in burns?'

'A dark magic spell that went wrong,' said Crazy Wolf solemnly. 'The Heng-Choke folk made the mistake of turning to the dark side thinking it would solve their problems but they have learned that it can only make things much worse.'

Jez sighed. 'I feel sorry for the parents of the missing kids. Who would do something like that?'

'I do too,' said Yenene. 'I'm kinda glad to be away from Big Belly though – he was starting to creep me out.'

Crazy Wolf grinned mischievously. 'I think Chief Big Belly was sending you some heart-shaped smoke signals there, my sister.'

★ ★ ★

We rode long and hard over the dusty terrain of the
Wastelands until up ahead I saw the outline of Fort
Westwood, the high stockade fence and lookout tower.
Soon, we were riding up to the gate.

On entering the fort, the sentry spoke to Clint. Then
Clint, Jez and I were immediately ushered into Captain
Mortimer's office to find the High Sheriff seated there,
a look of concern on his face.

'I have some grave news,' he said. 'We've received
another threat note from Imelda.'

CHAPTER EIGHT

★

Xylas Phlum

I shivered as I caught sight of the blood-red ink on the envelope.

Opening it, the High Sheriff took out the note, similar to the first on tattered yellowing paper. But this time there was something else in there. It looked like a newspaper cutting. He read:

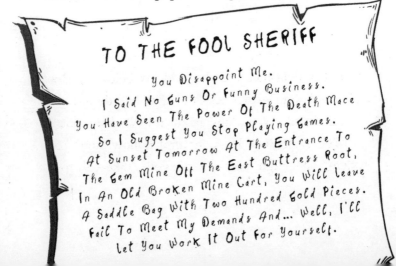

TO THE FOOL SHERIFF

You Disappoint Me.
I Said No Guns Or Funny Business.
You Have Seen The Power Of The Death Mace
So I Suggest You Stop Playing Games.
At Sunset Tomorrow At The Entrance To
The Gem Mine Off The East Buttress Root,
In An Old Broken Mine Cart, You Will Leave
A Saddle Bag With Two Hundred Gold Pieces.
Fail To Meet My Demands And... Well, I'll
Let You Work It Out For Yourself.

'There's a newspaper cutting,' he added.

'What's it say?' I asked.

The High Sheriff unfolded it.

The headline read:

ROOT COLLAPSE FROM STRUCTURAL DAMAGE COULD KILL HUNDREDS

But Imelda had added in red ink below it, 'Root Collapse From Death Mace Could Kill Hundreds.'

I frowned. 'What does she mean? What are roots?'

'The West Rock has a natural hollow stone root system,' the High Sheriff explained. 'Like the roots of a tree, there are big roots called buttress roots that divide into smaller offshoots, running below towns and villages, as well as under the city of Rockfoot.'

I felt my heartbeat quicken. 'So this time it looks like Imelda plans to explode a Death Mace not in the middle of a city but *under* a city.'

I saw a look of fear in the High Sheriff's eyes. He looked up, his eyebrows lowered in a frown. 'What an outrage! This evil wolfer is gonna try an' wipe out an entire city just like she tried at Edgewater.'

'But is this article accurate? I mean, who wrote it?' Jez asked.

'Troll by the name of Xylas Phlum. I read this article myself last week. In fact I sent a detachment to go see Phlum in Rockfoot and find out more about his claims but he weren't home – probably down in the roots.'

'Structural damage by what?' I asked.

The High Sheriff passed me the cutting. 'Mine axes.'

I read the article about how Phlum reckoned the gem miners, led by the greedy boss, Titus Knott, were weakening the natural foundations of the West Rock by chipping away at the insides of the roots. It documented how Phlum had carried out studies with the conclusion that if it continued, then it was only a matter of time before some of the roots collapsed. The article finished with Phlum stating he was pretty sure this greedy mine owner was not only destroying the rock but using illegal slaves, too.

'What do we do?' said Jez.

'Well, for a start, there's no time to return to Fort Mordecai,' said the High Sheriff. 'We have until sunset tomorrow to save Rockfoot or some other town from disaster. From now on we'll direct operations from Fort Westwood. Clint, you'll go visit Xylas Phlum in the morning. If he knows so much about the roots, maybe he's seen Imelda. Will and Jez, you will accompany Clint. I will organise a party to head to the gem mine and prepare for the drop. I'll need to speak to the mayor of Rockfoot about possible evacuation, too.'

★ ★ ★

The next morning, having got Xylas Phlum's address from the High Sheriff, Clint, Jez and I rode to the troll's pit house on the outskirts of the city. Uncle Crazy Wolf and Yenene were going to fly back up to Mid-Rock City.

A pit house, as the name suggests, is made by digging a house-sized hole in the ground then building a roof over the top, using branches and mud then adding a long thin chimney to poke out of the roof into the sky. Seeing it reminded me of Dugtown, a whole town of pit houses up on the eastern arm that I used to visit a lot when I lived with Grandma.

I knocked on the door.

No answer.

'He ain't home,' said Jez.

I looked at Clint. 'Do we come back later?'

'Ain't time. An' I'd really like to take a look around. Jez, can you get us in there?'

Jez picked the lock of the wooden door, opened it and made sure to close it behind us. We walked down a steep staircase into Xylas Phlum's house. A faint light flickered from deep below, but it was still quite gloomy.

112

I called out, 'Is anyone home?'

As I did my foot caught something and I heard a clunk. I looked up as an enormous rearing underbear fell towards me. Teeth flashed and fearsome clawed paws struck my shoulders, pushing me over as the beast pinned me to the ground. Cold fear jabbed at my heart like a frozen arrow tip. Jez screamed. A rifle cracked. Then quickly I realised all was not as it seemed. The bear wasn't moving. And instead of being soft and warm, the bear felt cold and rigid. It was dead, long dead. It was a stuffed trophy like the kind Imelda used to keep in her cave.

A rifle cocked in a dark corner of the room.

'Hands in the air, real slow,' a voice growled.

Clint and Jez both put up their hands.

'I'm a soldier,' Jez blurted out. 'The sky cavalry.'

'An' I'm the High Sheriff!'

'Quite a coincidence.' Clint grinned. 'Seeing we saw the High Sheriff only this morning back in Fort Westwood.'

I craned my neck to see past the bear's shoulder and saw a bald, lumpy-faced troll appear from the gloom, slowly moving forwards to peer at Captain Clint.

113

He nervously looked him up and down. Face reddening, the troll inspected Jez then lastly me, sprawled under the stuffed bear and finding it more and more difficult to catch a breath under its heavy bulk.

'Well, I'll be a— The sky cavalry!' The troll lowered the rifle barrel. He cleared his throat, coughing up a mouthful of phlegm which he spat into a fireplace. I felt relieved as I figured he was probably a rattlethroat troll, not a snake belly. I couldn't see any snakes wriggling under his shirt. 'You'll excuse me, ain't bein' inhospitable, 's just ya can't be too careful.'

'Not these days you can't,' Clint agreed. 'Rock can be a dangerous place if you don't keep your wits about ya. We're looking for Xylas Phlum.'

'Then ya found him.'

'I'm Captain Clint. Myself and Privates Jez and Gallows have got some questions for you.'

I was starting to worry they might all sit down for a nice cup of coffee while I got slowly squashed to death by this stupid giant fur ball. 'Help!' I managed to croak, clapping my hand to the animal's brawny back.

Jez struggled with it until Phlum used his spade-sized hand to assist her and easily lifted the bear off me.

The troll grinned. 'Reckon Big Joe likes ya, soldier.'

I got to my feet, dusting down my uniform. 'I'm just glad Big Joe ain't breathing.'

'I didn't skin 'em y'know. I couldn't – I hate the sight of blood. He's an old exhibit from Rockfoot museum; I was curator there a few years back.'

Xylas Phlum was a short, fat troll with a bald head, bulbous nose and big ears that any elf would've been proud of. He wore a brown bark-cloth tunic and his voice was rasping, typical of a rattlethroat.

I looked around Phlum's living room. It was cluttered with junk. There were bookcases stuffed with old books and newspapers, plus a cabinet full of bottles and packets: Pinkhurst's Herbal Medicine, Clattersnake Oil and Kickapee Blood and Stomach Restorer. When I was little, Pa had told me about these medicines. They were sold as wonder cures by crooks in suits when they were really nothing more than a few herbs and spices mixed with oil and water. Beside the cabinet there was a table strewn with pieces of rock and a magnifying glass, and wooden display cases with all kinds of insects and moths impaled on pins.

'Where did you get all this stuff?'

'Studyin' rocks an' collectin' bugs bin a hobby o' mine since I was a kid.'

Following my gaze, Phlum lifted one of the cases. 'See that charred grub that looks like it's been kicked out of a sky cowboy's camp fire – you'd never think to look at it but it turns into the most beautiful butterfly on the whole of the rock.'

'Ya ever caught one?' I asked.

'No chance. As well as bein' beautiful, it's got wings on it like a windhorse. Why, it's gotta be the fastest bug on the rock. Anyways, I take it you folk ain't here to see my bug collection?'

Clint took out the press cutting of Phlum's article from the *Mid-Rock City Times* Imelda had sent, turning it round so Phlum could see it.

'How certain are you about the weakening of the buttress root with the possibility of offshoots collapsing below towns and cities?'

'I'm convinced of it. As well as studyin' bugs an' rocks, I been studyin' the roots for years.'

Rummaging in the bookcase, Phlum brought over a photograph. It was a picture of a row of town buildings, a saloon and other stores that had all collapsed into a wide crevice in the ground.

'Picture was taken after a gem mine collapsed, swallowing up most of the town of Firestone out by the West Woods. Wondered how long it was gonna be before the cavalry started taking an interest.'

'We're taking more than an interest. We got us a huge problem.'

'I don't understand.'

'Dunno if you heard 'bout the explosion on the Flyer?'

Phlum nodded. 'Yeah, read about it in the paper. Seemed like a lotta destruction. What the heck happened there?'

'A mad wolfer called Imelda Hyde has invented a deadly new weapon called a Death Mace. Looks like a mace, only it's a lot more powerful. That's what completely destroyed the train carriage, leaving a barn-sized crater in the ground. We managed to de-couple the carriage before the whole train rolled into town, or folk would've been killed.'

Phlum's jaw dropped open.

'We ain't told the press what really happened for fear of spreading panic,' Clint went on, 'plus we ain't sure what the Death Mace actually is. All we know is that it contains a mixture of elf magic and traditional weaponry. Anyway, our problem is that this wolfer is now threatening to detonate one of these Death Maces inside a root offshoot below a town or city at sunset unless we pay a ransom.'

'That's downright madness. Ten people lost their lives in Firestone.'

'Can you help us? High Sheriff will pay you for your time, of course.'

'How can I help?'

'You know the roots better than any of us in the sky cavalry. We could do with your expertise in figuring out a way of stopping Imelda before it's too late.'

'Sure I'll do what I can – but y'ain't got much time – y'said by sunset this evenin' and it's around noon now.'

'That's why there ain't a moment to lose. We think she might even be hiding down there.'

'If she is, she'd need to be able to look after herself. She'd need to know her way around and be pretty fearless, too.'

'Why?'

'Roots ain't the kinda place for the faint-hearted. There are more skeletons down there than Rockfoot bone orchard.'

Phlum sighed. 'The skeletons are folk who ventured down, maybe prospectin' for gold or gems or huntin' or for curiosity, then got lost and eaten by underbears or had their souls sucked out by a wraith.'

I shivered.

'Another thought is that maybe she's manufacturing these Death Maces somewhere down there.'

'Could be. Plenty o' nodules down in the roots.'

'Nodules?'

'Pull up a pea plant and examine the roots and you'll see little lumps on 'em,' Phlum explained, 'some pretty tiny but others as big as your thumb. It's the same down there, some of the roots got caverns runnin' off 'em. Most of them are no bigger than my pit house but a couple are quite large.'

I thought of Imelda's lair back in the hollow hills.

'Big enough to hide a wolfer's deadly magic for making weapons?' Clint quizzed.

'It's possible.'

'The drop point is at the Knott Gem Mine entrance. Is there any way we could stage an ambush, say hide some troops inside the entrance to pounce on Imelda during the drop?'

Phlum nodded. 'Ya ever seen a map o' the roots?'

'No.'

Striding to the fireplace, Phlum pulled a string, unrolling a chart down the wall. It looked like a picture of a tree trunk shown side on with roots snaking below ground level.

'This here's a cross-section of the roots. The roots are like chokewood tree roots that extend both below and above ground at intervals: above ground they appear as low hills. Each buttress root splits into smaller root systems called offshoots. It's inside one of these that the gem miners have hacked out their quite extensive gem mine, weakenin' the natural root linin'.

As well as hewin' out the ore to sift for gems, they also widen them for their mine carts. Titus Knott knows to keep his mouth shut for fear they'll close the mine down.'

Clint studied the map. 'OK, so the plan is we go check out these offshoots and nodules to see if we can find Imelda or where she's making the Death Maces. Failing that, we make our way over to the gem mine to check out possible ambush points.'

'You mentioned payment,' said Phlum. 'How much ya talkin'?'

'Five gold pieces,' said Clint.

Phlum stroked his chin. 'Can get pretty dangerous down there. How 'bout stretchin' that to fifteen?'

'Ten. Five now and another five when the job's done.'

The haggling was interrupted by the crack of a rifle coming from outside.

'Y'in there Xylas Phlum?' a gruff voice shouted. 'We'd like a word with ya 'bout some of the stuff you been tellin' the papers!'

'Slavers!' Phlum breathed. Wiping the sweat from his brow, he pounced on a bottle of Cure All and took a long swig. 'I knew they'd find me. I'm doomed. Slavers don't take kindly to anyone from down here who don't see their way o' things.'

I remembered the newspaper article saying that Phlum was pretty sure a greedy mine owner was not only destroying the rock but using illegal slaves, too.

'Seen some bad stuff down there,' Phlum explained. 'Guards carryin' whips – I figure they ain't just to keep folk out, but to keep the workers in!'

Phlum, his hand trembling, took another swig of Cure All. Upstairs, the unseen rifle barrel blazed again, blasting through the door. Bullets ricocheted down into the room.

'Go away! Leave me alone!' he yelled, his voice quavering.

Clint removed his pistol. 'I ain't standing for this. 'Gainst the law to threaten folk, especially in their own home – I'm going up there. Will, Jez – you stay here.'

Phlum scuttled over to stand in his way. 'With all due respect, Captain, I wouldn't advise it 'less ya wanna a bullet in the chest. Them folks don't care who they shoot. Not all rock bottom folk are as hospitable as me.' He grabbed an old saddle bag off a peg attached to the banister. 'I have another suggestion.'

'What?'

'First, ya got yerself a deal – ten gold pieces.' He filled the bag with a map of the roots, beef strips, water containers and bottles of Cure All. Hurrying to a corner of the room, he drew back a velvet curtain, exposing what looked like a metal cage. 'Be a tight squeeze but should take four.' He glanced at Jez. 'Three and a half.'

'Take us where?' I asked.

Phlum took yet another swig of Cure All, then pulled back a metal cage door that squealed in protest.

'I bought this pit house a coupla years ago 'cos I knew it was built above an offshoot of the southern buttress root. Then I dug my own way into the roots. Took a heck of a lot of diggin' but it was worth it as saves me havin' to make the journey to the nearest cave entrance outta town. This lift will take us straight down and from there we can start lookin' for this crazy wolfer.'

Clint gasped, 'You mean that rusty ol' jail cage can descend all that way underground safely?'

'Ain't got stuck yet, an' besides, ain't like ya got a whole list of other options right now.'

A blazing torch – a shaft of wood with a burning twisted straw at one end – clattered down the staircase, landing beside the underbear. The bear's fur caught fire, giving off thick black smelly smoke. Two more torches followed and smoke and flames began to spread quickly into the room. We were trapped. Clint's plan to face the outlaws had just gone up in smoke.

'My stuff!' Phlum choked, as it dawned on him that his home and all his belongings were about to be lost forever. 'Quick, help me get some of it into the lift.'

Phlum directed us to grab the big root map and butterfly cases and as much as we could carry to salvage it from the fire then, coughing and spluttering, we all hurried aboard the lift. Flames began to lick the velvet curtain.

With all of us safely inside, Phlum closed the cage door then pulled a lever. There was a terrific judder, followed by a grating clanking noise. Slowly we began to descend.

CHAPTER NINE

★

Menace in the Roots

What kind of dark place were we slowly descending to? I felt my heart thump faster under my shirt. Phlum sure hadn't painted too bright a picture of the roots, telling us about all the evil critters that lived there.

I thought about Moonshine. I hoped she would be OK up there in the strange surroundings with those slavers attacking the house. Especially in light of what Jez had said about the rock bottom being dangerous. Still, Shy could handle herself pretty well.

The lift started clanking even louder, like an old steam engine, and sounded like it might break down at any moment.

Obviously sharing my concerns, Clint asked, 'You

sure this thing is gonna make it?'

'Sure I'm sure,' said Phlum. 'Ain't got stuck yet.'

Jez wiped the sweat off her forehead then nodded down at the display cases we'd rescued from the flames. 'Be glad to get outta here, I feel like one o' those pinned bugs.'

I had something bigger on my mind. We'd escaped the flames but now I feared underbears would hear us coming and be waiting for us – that is, if we even made it down there.

Phoenix Creek and Oretown, the places where I'd grown up on the now-collapsed western arm, seemed so distant now. Apart from the occasional shoot out, the western arm had been a pretty safe place to live. But my pa had been right when he'd told me the West Rock got more dangerous the further down the rock you travelled.

Finally, the lift came to a halt with a jolt inside a dimly lit tunnel. I breathed a quiet sigh of relief. Without a word, Phlum opened the steel cage.

We had arrived in the roots.

The hunt for Imelda and her Death Mace armoury was on.

'Everybody OK?' Phlum asked.

The first thing to strike me was the air, cool and damp. It was dark, too, but when my eyes adjusted I noticed colourful light radiating from some parts of the root tunnel walls and roof. I was familiar with the purple saddlewood light of Deadrock cavern, having spent some time down there a while ago, but down here there was a rainbow of colours: deep greens and blues, rich reds and golden yellows. It reminded me of bright sunlight striking a waterfall.

'Are *you* OK, Phlum?' I said, suddenly aware that he looked pretty shook up. After all, he'd just seen his place go up in smoke.

He put a big shovel hand on my shoulder. 'I'm fine. And thanks. Just set the stuff from the house anywhere round here an' I'll get to it sometime. Guess I'll be lookin' for a new place in Rockfoot but I can't worry 'bout that now.'

'Where's that light coming from?' I asked.

'The rock itself glows, well ain't really the rock but the minerals inside the rock,' Phlum explained.

'It's beautiful,' said Jez. 'Ain't ever seen somethin' so purty. I guess the gems are found inside this colourful rock.'

Phlum shook his head. 'Not so. Ya could hack this rock till the cows come home and you wouldn't find so much as a splinter of a gem. It's the black drab rock of the eastern offshoots that yields the best treasure – where the slaves are minin' as we speak.'

I frowned. 'But wouldn't folk want to buy glowing rock just as much as gems?'

A pile of tools lay at the lift entrance and Phlum handed me a pickaxe. 'Go ahead.'

'What?'

'Take a chunk out of it.'

I swung the axe deep into the rock face. A chunk of rock broke away and as it did the colour, a rich glowing red, gradually began to fade. My mouth dropped open.

'What happened?'

'Once the rock leaves the root wall or ceiling its colour dies. It conducts the light from the root as a whole and so when it breaks off, the colour fades.'

'It's magic,' I said.

'Roots are full o' magic, I've learned that over the years.'

'Amazing,' said Clint. 'I'm beginning to realise

why you enjoy studying it so much.'

'Well, now we all got accustomed to the light,' Phlum began, 'reckon we should get a move on. To recap then: the plan is to search for where the crazy wolfer, Imelda, might be hiding out or building these Death Mace weapons. If we can't find her then as your captain says, we'll make our way over to the gem mine for the rendezvous.' He heaved a deep breath. 'Well now, in order to do all this, reckon it's time for me to introduce you to the mode of transport down here.'

Phlum gestured to a gloomy corner where the rock seemed to have none of the special glowing minerals. And I saw two eyes like ink pots, glistening in the darkness, peering over at us. The biggest bat I'd ever set eyes on was hanging upside down from the root roof, wings folded over its body like it was holding an overcoat tightly against the wind. My heart raced.

Phlum whistled and it spread its wings which spanned about twice my size and ended in clawed hands. Then it dropped from the roof with a swishing noise and a gust of wind from those magnificent wings. It swooped towards me and over my head, disappearing far into the cave. Looking back, I saw there were more

131

bats, a whole family of them, gawking at me from the corner of the cave. Next thing a slightly smaller bat dropped from the roof and went speeding after the other. Moments later they both reappeared to land on the root floor near Phlum, folding their leathery wings awkwardly beside their furry bodies so they looked like kites that had crash-landed on a windy day.

Phlum grinned. 'Might I introduce you to the horse of the underground prairies.'

I recalled seeing Imelda jump off the Flyer carriage roof, cloak billowing behind her. I thought of the dark winged shadow that had swooped alongside the carriage as she fell. At first I'd thought it looked like a black windhorse but the wing span had been twice as wide as any horse's. Now I knew what it had been.

'Bats,' Jez stated.

'Root bats to be precise, seldom seen above ground so I'll forgive yer puzzled expressions. Dunno what I'd do without them. There are seriously big distances down here. Almost abandoned my studies before I even got started when I realised it were no place for horses.'

'Why ain't it good for horses?' I queried.

'Too uneven. Horse would break a leg on the

potholes, crags and uneven floor. That's if you don't gallop over the edge of a descendin' root offshoot and plunge to your death.'

'What about a winged horse?' I asked.

'The visibility down here is too poor for a winged horse. The roots ain't like the regular tin mines of Deadrock, with saddlewood branches littered everywhere. What little light there is comes from the luminous minerals embedded in the root rock.'

'Might be an idea for the cavalry,' Clint grinned. 'If there was a shortage of windhorses. Be great for night patrol.'

'Root bats can fly in the darkest, gloomiest parts of the roots and don't tire easily either, which is good for longer flights.'

I thought of Moonshine. 'Bit like my windhorse. She could fly to the top of the West Rock without grumbling.'

'So how do we mount them?' asked Jez.

'Same way as a horse.' Phlum mounted the biggest bat, sitting just behind its head. 'I'll take the captain if one of you two reckon you can handle the other. You won't have to do much, he'll follow his pa anyway. So we'll be takin' the lead.'

I stepped over the folded wing. The bat tilted its head to peer at me with a black beady eye, ears twitching. It opened its mouth, letting out a deafening screech. I noticed it had sharp teeth. Phlum had a loose leather collar like a horse's bridle fitted to the bat with reins. I clung to them.

The bat used its big talon-like thumb on the tip of its wing to help it leap into the air.

And we were airborne. Jez let out a scream and clung tighter to my waist.

I gripped the reins as our root bat picked up speed, the veins in its black leathery wings pulsing as it flapped vigorously, propelling us along the tunnel.

Shy didn't have such a hairy back and huge pointy ears or make ear-piercing screeching noises.

We swooped around the corner then into a much larger tunnel with side passages branching off to the left and right.

'This is the main southern buttress,' Phlum called back. 'We're directly under the bottom of the West Rock, roughly below the entrance to Deadrock.'

We chased on through the tunnel. The magical glowing rock was a blur of striking colour, punctuated by moments of blackness you could almost feel. I kept my eyes peeled for any sign of Imelda but as time went by I began to realise that finding anything or anybody down here wasn't going to be easy. I got more than a few mouthfuls of what felt like spider webs in these darker pockets of the root and had to spit them out. Once I felt something crawling on my neck and swiped off a huge spider. It landed on the bat's head and I brushed it off again.

Phlum and Clint disappeared down a smaller root, Phlum yelling, 'I'm gonna take a shortcut over to the eastern buttress. There's a place called the Ghole Cavern might be worth checking out. Follow me.'

Then I saw Phlum slow down and bring his bat down to land with a flurry of dust.

Eyes adjusting to the gloom, I saw why. The tunnel was a dead end, completely blocked up by a wall of broken boulders and rubble.

I landed my bat too but made a mess of it and both Jez and I tumbled off.

'This passage used to take you straight to the eastern buttress,' said Phlum, 'but the whole offshoot has collapsed. An' that ain't the first I've seen either. It's like I wrote about in my article. It's becomin' a problem.'

'Is there another way to the eastern buttress?' I asked, dusting myself down.

'Dozen. And all twice as long as this way. C'mon, we'll double back.'

Just then, I heard a loud roar and looked round to see a family of enormous underbears, like the one I'd been pinned underneath back at Phlum's house. Only this time they were alive and they looked hungry.

Dagger-sharp teeth flashed in the dim light. I quickly decided I preferred the stuffed version a whole lot better.

'Underbears!' cried Phlum.

I swallowed hard.

'Brings a whole new meaning to the phrase "dead end"!'

CHAPTER TEN

★

Goblin Slaves

The biggest underbear drew himself up to his full height – almost reaching the roof of the cavern. He roared, beating his claws on his black shiny-furred chest. His teeth were sabre-sharp and longer than a pick-tooth wolf's.

Clint unholstered his pistol.

'Be wastin' yer bullets,' Phlum advised. 'Underbears got hide tougher than a thunder dragon. Shootin' them only gets them even angrier and then they'll tear yer head off for sure.'

Jez wielded her bone-handled knife but Phlum just laughed.

I had an idea. 'I might be able to cause a bit of a diversion with some elf magic to hopefully buy us enough time to fly outta here.'

I took out a handful of magic leaves and crushed them up in my palm as I began chanting a spell in the elf tongue.

'Wampan obe hokan wimpawa!'

Gradually a windball began to form in my palm, cloudlike steam spinning furiously, growing steadily bigger. It whistled like a tornado, blowing off my cap and pinning my ears to my head. Finally, I unleashed it towards the advancing underbears. The windball – still expanding – streaked along the gloomy tunnel, colliding with the biggest underbear, sending it hurtling across the tunnel floor like a wooden bowling pin.

The other underbears roared, staggering backwards, stumbling and falling off their feet.

'C'mon, let's get outta here!' I cried.

We mounted our root bats, soaring past the dazed underbears. But the biggest underbear was on his feet again and swiped at my bat. I caught a glimpse of a huge clawed paw and felt a flash of pain in my ankle as it tried to grab me.

Onwards through the dark, twisting passageways we flew until Phlum yelled, 'We're in the eastern buttress now, near the gem mine. But more importantly these roots got the highest number of nodules in the entire network. I know time ain't on our side but it might be worth checking some of them out quickly.'

After a while Phlum veered off the main root into a gaping cavern and we landed our root bats to look around.

'They call this one the dragon's mouth cavern – one of the biggest caverns in the eastern buttress.'

It was a breathtaking place, lit like the rest of the roots with glowing colours from the magical, mineral-rich walls. Spindly stalactites drooped deep into the centre of the cavern with flowing contours that looked like melted wax. And where stalagmites rose to meet them, it had the appearance of gnashing, sharp teeth.

'Watch out, Will!' Jez cried and grabbed my arm as I was about to stumble into a hole in the ground.

Phlum came over. 'Meant to warn yez 'bout them.'

I gasped. 'What *are* they?'

Lifting a rock, Phlum tossed it down the hole. 'Descending root offshoots. Looks like a deep one, too. Been a long time 'fore we'd have heard you hit the bottom.'

I heard a faint thud coming from the hole and gulped.

Jez clenched a fist. 'I know who I'd like to toss in there instead of a rock – a smelly ol' wolfer.'

Phlum had a final look round then announced, 'Looks uninhabited. Reckon she ain't been here.'

At the cavern entrance, we were about to mount our root bats when I heard noises. Turning a corner, there was a sign:

KEEP OUT!
Our guards will shoot first and ask questions later!

KNOTT GEM MINE

A mine cart appeared from the gloom, pushed by a skinny goblin, gasping, cursing and hacking. His cart had a number on the front.

When he saw us he flinched, covering his head with his hands as though he thought we were going to strike him.

'Pardon us, stranger, but we ain't miners, we're soldiers passin' through,' I explained.

'Say, are you OK?' Jez asked.

The miner raised his eyes then blinked. 'S ... s ... soldiers ya say, come down 'ere – but why?'

'Glodd, we gotta get this lot down to the entrance,' said another goblin, ignoring us.

'Can we help?' offered Clint.

Glodd looked at him, eyes narrowed in a look of distrust. 'Master wouldn't like it. We'll be on our way.'

I was curious. 'How many of these carts must you fill in a day?'

'Ten.'

I gasped. The cart was quite large and to fill even one with heavy and hard-grafted ore would be backbreaking work. I felt sorry for the poor goblin miners.

'How much do you get paid?'

At first the goblin seemed hesitant, then he muttered, 'If we fill them all – we eat.'

'And if not?'

He didn't answer.

Just then I heard a scream. It seemed to come from round the corner. We went to investigate and I saw a poor goblin being lashed by a man carrying a whip.

'Aaaarggh!' the miner cried out, falling against the mine cart he'd been filling.

'This cart ain't even half full ya lazy lowlife,' the man yelled. 'Ya forget ya got a quota to meet?'

'I ain't forgot, sir, I'll make me quota. I swear. I'll make me quota,' the goblin whimpered.

The man, fat and bald with a beard shot through with grey hairs, cracked the whip again.

'Please, sir.'

'And what are you lot looking at?' he barked at two miners who'd stopped work to see what the commotion was. 'Get back to work or I'll flog the lot of you.'

'Stay your lash, mister,' yelled Clint. 'I think they get the message!'

The slaver spun round and pointed the rifle at us. 'What the...? Who the heck are you?'

'The sky cavalry, so you can lower that rifle. And who might you be?'

'Name's Knott, Titus Knott, owner of this here mine,' he spat. 'Can't say I'm happy 'bout you boys crawlin' like ants all through my mine, especially without me knowing about it.'

'As a captain in the sky cavalry, I don't need your permission – in fact, I reckon I'll be checkin' back pretty soon if this is the way you're treatin' these miners. Slavery's illegal now, y'know.'

145

'Ain't no slaves in my mine – all of them paid workers. Ain't that right, Gobrott?'

The goblin nodded, trembling.

I glanced at the whip Knott was trying to keep out of sight. 'Don't look that way to me.'

Clint glowered at him. 'You can be sure we'll be following this up.'

Phlum was right. Slavery was continuing in this mine and maybe others like it.

Knott growled. 'I saw more of your boys sniffin' about outside, what's goin' on?'

Clint looked at Jez and me. 'The party from Fort Westwood! We'll make our way there now to meet them.'

'So ya gonna tell me what this is all about?' asked Knott.

'Matter of security,' said Clint. 'You seen anyone acting suspiciously of late?'

He shook his head.

'We need to keep the mine entrance clear tonight after sundown for an hour – we have an operation to carry out.'

'Fine. Just don't be snoopin' around helping yourself to my ore.'

We made our way to the mine entrance. Hunched-over and exhausted-looking miners wheeled carts of ore over to water flumes then dumped the contents on the ground in piles. Titus Knott had followed us out and was busying himself checking the water supply to the flumes, where more miners sat washing the ore to sift out the gems. He kept disappearing in and out of his office – a wooden hut not far from the mine entrance. Didn't this mine ever close? I wondered.

I spotted the High Sheriff, who'd arrived with a company of soldiers. My heart lifted when I saw Moonshine among the tied-up horses and I hurried over to see her.

'Shy, ya got away from Phlum's then?'

'Just about. When those men showed up with shooters I took flight. I came back to look for you and when there was no sign I was so worried. How'd you get out?'

'We went underground. Phlum has a mechanical lift, took us straight down into the roots.' I gave her a pat on the neck. 'Drop time's approaching and things are bound to get

147

hostile when Imelda shows up. Sit tight and stay alert, Shy, and I'll speak to you soon.'

'Don't worry, I plan to. No rotten wolfer's gonna stop me passin' out this weekend.'

Outside of the mine, the High Sheriff assembled us to discuss the plan.

Approaching him, Clint saluted.

The High Sheriff mirrored the salute. 'Clint, Jez, Will. I'm glad you made it out safely. How did you get on?'

'Firstly, sir, I'd like to introduce you to Xylas Phlum.' Clint grinned. 'Phlum, this is the *real* High Sheriff.'

Face reddening, Phlum shook the High Sheriff's hand. 'Pleased to meet you, sir.'

'Howdy, Phlum – I appreciate you coming on board to help.'

'Be willin' to stick around and help with the drop if you can use me.'

The High Sheriff nodded. 'Then consider yourself deputised for the day.'

'We checked out the roots,' Clint explained, 'but there was no sign of Imelda. However we did uncover something just as ugly – Titus is definitely using slaves in this gem mine.'

'I knew it. We'll see to that when all this is over. Drop time's coming up. We gotta learn from our previous mistakes. This time we're gonna deploy men around the mine perimeter, a coupla miles away, two in close, then two in the mine. Imelda will have no chance. If she so much as breaks wind, we'll know about it.'

I smiled.

'Though we need to be covert, too – if Imelda senses anyone is about, she'll not go for the gold. We're not taking any chances so we got real gold this time. We want Imelda to grab it, thinking she's got away with it, then as she makes her escape, we pounce. I want you all to keep your eyes peeled. The Death Mace has the potential to do really serious damage with risk of massive loss of life. We must proceed with extreme caution.'

'Everyone take your positions. Will and Jez, I want you up on that rise. Clint, you'll position yourself a bit further out. I'll take Phlum inside the mine entrance.'

Glancing up at the sky, I saw that the sun was already starting to set.

Imelda would be on her way.

★ ★ ★

Time crawled by like a marsh slug, like always when you're waiting on something to happen.

'Where is she?'

Jez and I had taken up our positions on a hill overlooking the mine entrance and were waiting for Imelda.

In the twilight I saw a shadowy figure stagger down from the high ground, cloak billowing, a wide-brimmed hat on its head.

'It's Imelda,' I whispered to Jez.

'She's here then. You ready?'

'Yeah. Wait a minute, she's stopped.' I saw the figure crouch low to the ground like she'd stumbled.

'Get down, Will. She'll see you.'

'She's acting kinda weird.'

'Weird, what do you mean?'

'I'm pretty sure I saw her stumble on some rock, and I think she might have fallen over.'

'Maybe crouching, checking to see if any cavalry are lying in wait for her at the mine entrance.'

151

'Something ain't right.' I craned my neck. 'I can't see clear – I'm gonna take a look.'

'No, Will! The High Sheriff's orders are to stay put. You could blow the whole operation.'

'I won't. I just wanna get a bit closer to see what she's playing at. Ya coming?'

She shook her head. 'It ain't a good idea. We oughta stick together. As your mentor I want you to stay here.'

'I'll be OK, Jez. I promise I'll be back in the flick of a calf's tail.'

'That's an order, Will.'

I stared at her. 'Why are you actin' like this, Jez?'

'Actin' like what?'

'Like kinda bossy.'

'I ain't being bossy.  When you're a soldier, it's called giving orders.' Jez's face was reddening. 'I'm sure they've taught you that in your training. Besides, Captain Clint is somewhere 'bout there, if he'd seen anything, he'd have handled it – what makes you think you have to get involved?'

'I know I'm still a trainee, Jez, but I reckon it's my responsibility to be engaged in the mission.' I felt I could've done better the last time, on the roof of the Flyer. I felt I wanted to make amends.

'Disobeying orders ain't responsible, Will, it's dumb.'

'So, I'm dumb now.'

I quickly decided I didn't want to stick around and bicker with Jez. What I wanted to do was find out what Imelda was up to. Maybe I could nip things in the bud before she even got anywhere near the mine entrance. Make things easier for the High Sheriff. Stuff Jez just wouldn't understand.

Hearing Jez heave a sigh, I picked my way carefully over the scrub, using bushes and boulders for cover, like a hungry pick-tooth wolf closing in on its prey to where I was sure I'd spotted Imelda.

It *was* Imelda. I trod carefully, aware it may be a trap. She lay on the ground, completely still, wide-brimmed hat beside her. I drew my six shot and aimed it at her as I approached.

'Don't move, Imelda, or I'll shoot.'

She said nothing. She just lay there.

Edging closer, I noticed her dirty head bandages were covered in blood.

I kneeled beside her to examine them further, almost retching at the foul smell. I'd scarcely touched them when they loosened easily, falling off to reveal a cheek, a nose. The flesh the moonlight pulled from the gloom wasn't scarred or burned like I'd expected. It looked normal. The bandage loosened further to reveal a blood-spattered face.

Her hand grabbed my wrist, squeezing tightly and I froze with fear.

Then she gurgled, 'Will. Help me.' But it wasn't Imelda's voice.

The bloodied, wounded person underneath the bandages wasn't Imelda – it was Captain Clint!

CHAPTER ELEVEN

★

Deadly Magic

I swallowed a lump in my throat, and heard my breath quicken. My mind raced. What was Captain Clint doing wrapped in Imelda's bandages?

Of course, she'd stolen his uniform, but why? If Imelda wore no bandages what would she look like?

Clint had struck his head but was alive. He would live. I applied some magic herbs and uttered a healing spell as a terrible thought struck me like a mine pick striking a rock face. If Imelda had stolen his cavalry outfit then I had to get back to Jez real quick and warn her.

I stumbled blindly over the scrub back to the spot where Jez and I had been lying in wait, only to find she was gone. Frantically my eyes raked the hillside.

155

No sign. I searched around in case I'd got the wrong spot. No sign. Then, without wasting another second, I ran down the hill towards the mine entrance.

My heart pounded. Beside the old broken-wheeled cart at the mine entrance stood a thin figure dressed in cavalry uniform holding Jez, a forearm round her neck, a gun to her head. Holding her close like a dwarf shield. Imelda?

Dark hair tucked up into a soldier's cap. The sleeve of the jacket bore the stripes of an officer: a captain. The uniform was Captain Clint's. But could it now be on Imelda Hyde's body?

No. The face under the cap looked normal. There were no burn scars. It couldn't be Imelda. So, who was it?

I feared for Jez. If anything happened to her, I'd never forgive myself. This was all my fault. If I'd have listened to her when she said we should stick together maybe I could have protected her. But no, I had to rush off and try to solve the whole problem by myself, just like when I thought I could go after Noose Wormworx, the snake-bellied troll, and bring him in. Had I learned nothing?

What could I do? I thought about conjuring a fireball or a thunderball but both were far too risky and might hurt Jez or even kill her.

I was still thinking when the soldier boomed, 'All o' yez come out from your little rat holes with your hands held high, orders o' Captain Hyde.' She grinned. 'Or this young soldier gets a bullet. You too, elf kid – I know you're up there. And don't be getting any magic ideas if you wanna see your liddle girlfriend alive.'

It was Imelda. But where were her scars? It didn't make sense.

'What part of "no cavalry" did yez all have trouble with this time?' Imelda fumed, her voice clearer now with no bandages to muffle the sound. 'Can't yez read?'

Impatiently, she kicked open one of the mine gates.

'Gonna count to five, then pull the trigger. One ... two...'

Eyes locked on Jez, I ran down the hill, tossing my gun at her captor's feet. 'Let her go, Imelda!'

'S'far enough kid. She waved the pistol at me then resumed the countdown. 'Three ... four ...'

The High Sheriff and Phlum appeared at the mine entrance and threw down their weapons. 'Stop. We're here. Take the gold. Only let the soldier go,' said the High Sheriff.

'Getting kinda tired with you not following my orders,' Imelda went on, ignoring his request. 'Especially when you know the devastation my new invention can cause. It's even more destructive than the stone spitter. Bet you'd like to get your grubby little paws on it, wouldn't you – well guess what, clattersnakes will slither in straight lines before I'll let you steal this weapon off me.'

She nodded into the broken mine cart, where the

bag of gold lay. 'I've inspected the gold and am glad to see you brought the real thing this time. Least you got that part right.'

The whole time she'd been talking I'd been staring at her face. It was the face of a middle-aged half-elf woman. There was no scarring, no burns, she looked normal. But those dark eyes were Imelda's. They hadn't changed.

'Y ... your face?'

'Told you if yez were gonna play games with me I'd always be one step ahead.'

'But how? I saw your scars, I...'

'To give you credit, kid, I got you to thank for my new look. Seeing the way you fixed my leg back in the hollow hills after I got shot by the Gatlans rekindled my interest in elf magic. Got me thinking about healing my burns. And the more I started getting back into elf magic, the more I got to thinking about making me some magic weapons.'

'We saw the rune marks on the Death Mace,' I said. 'They led us to Heng-Choke Village – we know you were there, Black Raven. Did you kill Dancing Snake?'

At first she looked surprised we had been to

Heng-Choke Village. Then she ran a hand over her chin, mouth curled in a half-smile. 'Dancing Snake was a fine mage, much better than your stupid uncle Crazy Wolf. She had power, vision. She knew I hated my skin, that I'd been enslaved by it for years. *You are in bondage to those bandages,* she would say. *I want to set you free. I want to give you new skin. There is a spell…*'

'A spell to conjure skin? Uncle Crazy Wolf ain't ever told me about that.'

'Your uncle knows nothing of the power of dark magic,' she hissed.

'Go on,' said the High Sheriff.

'We went out by the river. Dancing Snake set a roaring fire, dusting it with magic leaves till it sparked and crackled. The sky was torn in two by lightning amid heavy clouds. Her eyes wide, she began to utter a spell in the elf tongue.'

I glanced at Jez, whose face was reddening from Imelda's arm round her neck. The High Sheriff stood, teeth clenched, glancing at Phlum, a look of powerlessness on his face.

'She clasped her hands on mine and soon her skin began to glow. Her eyes shone like stars as she entered

160

a trance. Then suddenly, a hot fork of lightning jabbed at our joined hands. The pain was excruciating. I fell backwards, yelling, nursing my stinging hands, noticing the bandages had been all but incinerated by the lightning. I expected to see fresh burns. But there were none. My burn scars were gone. My hands were just like they'd been before the accident in Gung-Choux Village.

'But something weren't right. The magic must have corrupted even though Dancing Snake had done everything right. No spell book can explain it, but sometimes magic can go wrong – terribly wrong.'

'What happened?' I urged.

'I looked up to see Dancing Snake covered in burns – it was like looking into a mirror. The healing spell had restored me but at the expense of Dancing Snake.'

'Couldn't you reverse it?' Phlum asked.

'She was yelling something about that but I

couldn't ... I liked my new skin. For the first time in years I felt like a person and not some freak. Finally I was free of those despicable dirty bandages.'

Imelda's face split in an evil grin. 'Dancing Snake must've seen my expression of revulsion and rushed to the river to gaze at her reflection. Her scream will haunt me to the day I die. In her distress she lost her balance and fell in the river. She cried for help but...'

I gasped. 'You ... you let her drown?'

'Can't swim.'

The High Sheriff gasped. 'So you fled the village.'

'I'd learned a lot, enough to help me with my new idea for a powerful weapon.'

Suddenly the sky darkened and I felt a rush of wind, accompanied by an ear-piercing screech. A root bat almost took my head off diving to land at Imelda's feet.

'Perfect timing, my furred friend.'

With an evil grin, Imelda forced Jez to mount the bat then climbed on behind her, the gun wedged in Jez's back. 'I'd like to stick around, but my work here is done.' She put a hand to her cavalry cap in salute then laughed. 'So this soldier's officially on leave with full pay.' She held the bag of gold tightly.

'Let the dwarf go, Imelda, you got what you wanted.'

'The private comes with me, call it a little insurance policy. Dunno why, but I don't trust yez – figure you might have a mind on following me.'

The root bat took to the air in a flurry of dust and grit.

'No!' I cried. I ran and leaped like a wood panther at the ascending bat, only just managing to grab hold of one of its scrawny back legs.

The bat shrieked and flapped its leathery wings faster, veering down a root tunnel to try and shake me off. I couldn't hold on for much longer. But with my last ounce of strength I let one hand go, at the same time conjuring a fireball that I directed at Imelda's back. I missed but the fireball struck the bat's wing and it shrieked with pain, tumbling from the air. I let go a heartbeat before the bat hit the ground, throwing its passengers rolling across the floor of the mine. Scrabbling to my feet, I noticed that Imelda was injured. Her head was cut and blood ran down her face. She was fumbling around the ground for her weapon. Seizing my chance, I leaped to my feet and pounced on her gun first. I pointed it at her. Jez was beside me, knife in hand.

'Don't look at her, Jez,' I warned. 'In case she tries that hypnotise spell on ya.'

'Heck, what did the cavalry do before you two joined up!' Imelda sneered.

'Think I preferred your bandages, least they filtered your rotten breath.'

Clenching a fist, she rose to her feet.

'Any closer an' I'll shoot,' I warned.

'Wouldn't shoot a soldier, now, would ya?' Imelda grinned, dusting down her cavalry shirt.

She felt her bleeding face. 'Hope that doesn't scar my pretty new face, kid, or I'll be mighty angry with you.'

I heard the sound of a rifle cock behind me, then a voice in the gloom. 'Drop your weapons and put your hands in the air!'

CHAPTER TWELVE

★

Tunnel of Treachery

I spun round and gasped. It was Eli Wynchester.
I frowned, eyeing the rifle barrel. 'Eli ... what in spirit's name are you doing here?'

'Drop the weapon.'

I let the gun fall to the ground.

'You look surprised,' he went on. 'You shouldn't be. But then like so many you haven't been looking closely enough. You've been too busy looking at the surface of things to really see what's going on underneath.'

'Bit like how folk been seeing me these last few weeks,' Imelda added with a grin.

'Quit talkin' in riddles, Eli – spit it out. What's goin' on?'

'Oh I'll spit it out all right. Me and my clever partner

here planned this whole extortion racket together.'

'Partner?' I gasped.

Imelda grinned. 'Ain't just a pretty face.'

'So you didn't tell Imelda you had no jobs – you hired her?'

He nodded. 'Imelda had the weapons skills I needed to pull the Wynchester factory back from the brink of bankruptcy. And I got me some gambling debts need paying.'

Jez fumed. 'So the Death Mace ain't made down here, it's made at your factory?'

'Oh, didn't I show you? I must've skipped that room on our little guided tour yesterday. We've kinda set up home there, too, though don't be expecting an invite for dinner.'

'You're rotten to the core, Eli Wynchester,' I spat. 'Your pa was a just man. Why, he'd turn in his grave if he knew you'd cooked up an extortion racket.'

'When you fall on hard times, sometimes being "just" doesn't cut it any more. Pa would've understood.'

I was gobsmacked. 'You'd let innocent folk die just so you can make a fortune in gold?'

'That's business, boy.' He turned to Imelda. 'C'mon, this place gives me the creeps, let's get outta here.'

'What do we do with them?' Imelda hissed.

'Shoot them. I passed one of those offshoot holes not far from here, we'll dump them down there.'

I gasped. 'What – I … they'll find us, you can't…'

Eli's pistol echoed in the narrow root tunnel and Jez crumpled to the floor.

I felt my whole body go numb. 'No!' I screamed.

Eli looked on coldly. Retrieving her gun from the root floor, Imelda pointed it at me. 'Goodbye, elf kid,' she said. 'Seems it weren't such a good idea after all, joining the sky cavalry – you shoulda stuck to riding thunder dragons and bending arrows in Gung-Choux Village.'

I heard a loud bang, and my world went black.

★ ★ ★

I opened my eyes as a stagecoach ran over my head, least that's what it felt like. The rest of me ached, too. Quickly I figured out I was too sore to be dead so I must be alive. But how? Imelda had shot me in the chest and Imelda don't usually miss. I moved my fingers to where my chest hurt a bit, expecting to feel blood but there

168

was none. Then I realised why. I felt a dent in the metal scorpion pendant Jez gave me. The bullet had struck the pendant and saved my life.

Blinking, I saw something glint above my head. It was shiny metal – a knife.

'Jez,' I croaked.

'He's awake,' came a voice.

The knife jabbed closer. 'Are you a guard?'

Swathed in the dim purple glow of a distant saddlewood lamp, a group of elf faces, kids mostly, clustered round me, staring. There was the noise of rattling chains.

'No. I'm Will Gallows, of the sky cavalry. Who are you?'

I thought about fighting but realised I was still far too groggy to put up much of a battle. I could barely focus.

'He don't look like a guard.'

'He ain't old.'

'Older than us.'

'Never seen a guard wear a uniform before.'

The kid lowered the knife and helped me to sit up. 'Look. We ain't gonna hurt ya. We're miners.'

'There was a girl,' I croaked, 'a dwarf girl with me…'

'Over there.' One of them pointed across the cavern. 'We heard shooting up in the mine, and next thing you two were thrown down here. What's going on?'

'I gotta see her.'

Groggily, I crawled over to Jez and the elf who was trying to help her.

'I tried to stop the bleeding. She's hurt pretty bad, a bullet I think.'

I examined her. Eli had caught her plumb in the shoulder. He might have been good at making guns but luckily for Jez he was no expert in firing one.

'Who applied this dressing?'

'I did,' said a little elf girl.

'You probably saved her life, thank you.'

Taking the last of my healing herbs, I sprinkled some on the wound. The bullet was still in there but I'd have to leave it for the doctors in Mid-Rock City Hospital.

Jez opened her eyes. 'Will, what's going on?'

'Everything's gonna be OK.'

'Where are we?'

I looked at the elf kid.

'You both tumbled into our prison,' he explained.

'Y'mean, you live down here?'

One kid lifted the heavy chain he was shackled to. 'Ain't like we're going anywhere.'

'Slaves,' I breathed.

'Can you get us out of here?'

I stared at the kids, noticing the dirty marks on their faces were actually forming elf face painting. And in the centre of the cavern they had carved a stalagmite into the shape of a totem pole. A thought suddenly struck me.

'Wait a sec – you kids know Heng-Choke Village?'

No answer.

'Look, we're not guards and we're nothing to do with Titus Knott or his rotten mine, and yes, we can get you outta here.'

'They took us at night,' the little girl who'd helped Jez blurted out. 'While our mothers and fathers slept and carried us away on great bats to this spirit-forsaken place.'

'So you *are* the elf kids from Heng-Choke.' Jez was now sitting up, the colour rising in her cheeks. 'Your chief told us of your kidnapping only yesterday.'

One by one, with a little careful magic, I released the children from their shackles.

'Jez, you OK to make a move?'

'Yeah, let's get outta here.'

Climbing out the hole wasn't too hard, though Jez needed some help. She'd lost blood and was pretty weak. Then we started out along the root tunnel. We hadn't journeyed far when I stumbled upon a guard lying motionless on the mine floor.

I kneeled to examine him.

'Is he dead?' Jez asked.

'Yeah. Most likely Eli's handiwork.'

We were almost out when I saw a shadow up ahead. A fat, bald man with a greying beard strode out of the gloom. He carried a whip and spotting us, cracked it loudly.

It was Titus Knott.

'Where the heck ya think you're going?' he hissed.

'You stole these kids from Heng-Choke Village, didn't ya?' I cried. 'To make them work down here as slaves!'

'Not just me, kid, but my pa before me. We've been rustling the kids of Heng-Choke Village for years.' He grinned. 'Ore don't mine itself y'know – we had to keep the mine stocked with fresh, hard-working slaves.'

'Well, it ends here, Titus,' said Jez. 'We're releasing them, on the authority o' the High Sheriff.'

'Authority o' the High Sheriff – pah! Inside this mine, I'm the only authority, 'specially when you bin goin' around murderin' my guards.'

I gasped. 'We didn't murder anyone.'

He noticed my ears. 'Well now, looky here, an elf soldier. Why, I should shackle you along with these kids here – make you dig me some ore.' He glanced at Jez and grinned. 'Got some narrow offshoots your friend could mine, so she don't feel left out.'

'We're releasing these young 'uns and bringing you in for questioning about kidnapping and illegal slavery.'

'Over my dead body.'

I glared at him. 'If that's what it takes.'

'Big talk from a soldier with no weapon that I can see.'

I considered a fireball but the kids were way ahead of me. Then one of them launched a stone at Titus, striking him in the chest. Titus groaned and fired his six shot into the air.

'Get back in the mine or I'll flog the lot of you!'

But the kids weren't frightened. It was like they'd got a taste for freedom and weren't going to let some fat slaver stand in their way. This time they hurled a volley of stones, one of which struck Titus in the forehead. And he fell flat on his face on the mine floor.

'Great shot, kid. C'mon let's get outta here.'

We hurried past him, out of the mine and met the High Sheriff, Phlum and a weary-looking Captain Clint. They were hunched over Phlum's map.

'Will, Jez! Thank goodness you're both OK, we're trying to figure out where you mighta got to,' said the High Sheriff. Then he stared at Jez's uniform. 'Jez, you're bleeding, what happened?'

'Bullet wound. Will applied a field dressing with some elf magic, so I'm OK.'

Phlum said, 'We searched inside for a while but there was no sign – where were you?'

'You wouldn't have found us, we were dumped down a hole, and that's where we met this lot.'

'Wow, who are all these children?'

'The elf kids from Heng-Choke. It was Titus's men who captured them and forced them to work down the gem mine.'

'Well, I'll be… We'll get them back to the fort then on to their village. Where's Titus?'

'In the mine – out stone cold.' I grinned, giving the elf kids a thumb's up. 'And there's more news – Imelda is at the Wynchester factory.'

The High Sheriff frowned. 'The factory – but how do you know?'

'You won't believe this, but Eli and Imelda are a couple. Eli showed up in the mine – he'd been shadowing Imelda. He's in this up to his neck so he can make a bundle and keep the factory from bankruptcy.'

'Eli and Imelda? Why the low-bellied scum…'

'They're both probably headed back to the factory with the gold.'

'Then we'll head there too, immediately. There ain't a moment to lose. I want those two rotten crooks behind bars before this day's out.'

CHAPTER THIRTEEN

★

Lethal Spirits

Moonlight bathed the Wynchester factory in pale ghostly light and it looked even creepier with its two tall chimney stacks towering up to the stars like wraith horns. And behind it, towering even farther into the sky, was the Great West Rock itself.

It was good to be riding Moonshine again and as we went I updated her on all the news about Imelda and Eli.

I glanced over at Jez in her blood-stained uniform. She looked kinda pale.

'You OK, Jez?'

'Quit worrying, I'm fine.' She smiled. 'Prairie dwarves are the toughest folk on the rock.'

As we neared the factory, the High Sheriff raised a hand.

'Listen up. If you thought the gem mine was dangerous, then this could be even worse. We got no idea what we're riding into here so I want you all to keep your eyes peeled for any sign of life. I want to find Imelda and Eli, and the part of the factory they're making the Death Mace in, so we can shut it down.'

'Do we have a plan?'

'There's no time, Eli and Imelda could be making their getaway right now,' said the High Sheriff. 'Y'all got training for a siege situation, so let's just get in there and see what's going on and if they're in there – flush them out.'

'And if they resist?' Clint asked.

'Shoot 'em.'

Phlum swallowed hard. 'There'll be blood, won't there?' His voice quivered. 'I hate blood.'

'You don't have to come, Phlum.'

'Y'said I was deputy for the day an' the day ain't over yet.' He grinned. 'I wanna help bring these two outlaws to justice.'

We approached the factory from the rear. I figured there was a good chance that's where Eli would be manufacturing the Death Mace, because on our last visit that was the part of the factory we hadn't seen.

It was dark but Clint had a few small saddlewood lamps among his supplies. We broke the locks and entered a long room. The main floor was littered with lathes and long wooden work benches, and an array of pulley wheels extended upwards to a balcony with more machinery. A conveyor belt with some pieces of metal on it ran up the middle of the room.

Then I noticed something. Partly concealed under a white sheet was a cylinder of iron, partially carved in the shape of a thunder dragon. A stone spitter. So Eli was making these weapons, too. I noticed a shadow lurking just behind the stone spitter.

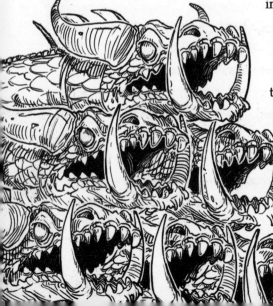

A light went on then a familiar voice said, 'You got more lives than a pack o' scrawny rock cats. How the heck you make it out of the gem mine alive?'

It was Eli. And standing next to him, a scowling Imelda Hyde.

I grinned. 'With the help of an iron scorpion and some elf kids.'

'This where you make the Death Maces?' Jez asked.

Eli nodded to a doorway. 'Room next to this one. Guns 'n' stone spitters in here.'

The High Sheriff announced, 'I'm bringin' you both in to stand trial for treason, attempted murder, extortion and a whole lot more.'

Eli burst out laughing. 'You stand in the middle of my weapons factory and threaten to bring us in. You have but a handful of guns. We have hundreds, not to mention stone spitters, which thanks to you, we can't sell for love nor money.'

'Yeah, do you really think we're going to come without a fight?' Imelda rasped. 'You got lucky in the roots, but you won't make it out of this factory alive.'

Eli pulled back a sheet, revealing a partially-built

181

stone spitter. He lit the fuse.
All three barrels exploded and
boulders hurtled towards us.

I dived for cover as one of the
boulders crashed into the pulley
system just above me. I covered my
head with my hands as bits of wood

and metal rained down. To my horror, I
realised that half of the soldiers who had
been deployed with us, along with
Clint, had taken the full brunt of the
boulders and lay dead or badly injured.

I couldn't see Jez. My mind went
numb. Had she been hit too? It was
more than I could take to think of her
lying dead under that rubble. I'd nearly
lost her once today, I couldn't bear it if rescuing
her had been for nothing and I'd lost her for good. My
eyes scanned the factory till I spotted she'd taken cover
behind a pillar. I breathed a deep sigh.

The High Sheriff gave the order to return fire
and the factory erupted in deafening gunfire. Six shot
and rifle barrels flashed, smoke billowed, and sparks

jumped as bullets ricocheted off machinery. Things looked dreadful – the casualties were horrific.

Imelda had taken cover but Eli stood grinning like a cat then pulled a cord. To one side of us a beam of wood appeared with about ten rifles fixed onto it, spaced apart at regular intervals – all aimed at us.

Eli pulled another rope and the rifles – hooked up by an elaborate mechanical system – opened fire simultaneously, firing a barrage of bullets. More soldiers were struck down, falling to the floor.

'Gotta have security in my factory,' Eli roared.

'I'm gonna get closer, take them both out with fireballs,' I cried.

Jez had made her way over to me. 'No, Will, there are more of those rifle booby traps on the other side, I can see them.'

'I'm go—' I caught myself remembering what happened the last time I disobeyed an order from Jez. 'OK, private, but we gotta do something.'

She grinned. 'We are, you're gonna get closer and take them out with fireballs—'

'But I just said that…'

183

'—After I get up there and cut the ropes to Eli's booby traps,' she finished.

'No way, Jez. That's suicide – you're still injured, remember. You'll never make it.'

'I'm small and hard to hit and I'm handier with a knife than you. Besides, I'm giving the orders.'

I grinned. 'I'll cover you.'

'Give me a foot up to that steel bar.'

And then Jez did something that took me by surprise. As I stooped, cupping my hands to give her a foot up, she kissed me lightly on the cheek. I felt my face redden and looked at her.

She smiled. 'For luck.'

I noticed her cheeks redden, too. 'It's a dwarf thing,' she added then propelled herself upwards to grab the bar, climbing up towards the roof of the factory.

It was Jez who was gonna need the luck as, spotting her, Eli opened fire, bullets sparking inches from where she climbed. I fired back and saw him duck for cover, buying Jez valuable seconds.

Crawling on her hands and knees like a Deadrock dust rat, Jez moved skilfully along the upper framework of the factory just below the balcony. Though more than a few times, I noticed her wince with the pain of her gunshot injury.

Eli was about to unleash another volley of rifle fire from above the rafters when Jez cut the rope. The beam of wood clattered to the ground. Eli clenched his fists in rage.

Imelda appeared and touched the fuse of the stone spitter and the three dragon heads roared, firing their deadly missiles. A boulder tore ferociously through the wooden support beam below where Jez was crawling and part of the balcony gave way.

'Jez, look out!' I yelled.

Jez clung frantically to the beam as it plummeted but lost her grip. She fell, landing on a conveyor belt. I heard Eli laugh then stride to what looked like a control panel with buttons and levers. He pulled a lever and the conveyor belt sprang to life and Jez – lying motionless – began to move towards Eli.

'Finish her off,' Imelda goaded her partner.

'Leave her to me,' he rasped.

Palms tingling, I crawled, staying low, towards the control panel. Injured soldiers littered the factory floor,

some trapped below fallen beams, and I saw the High Sheriff, his leg bloodied – he'd taken a hit. As Eli raised his gun, I conjured a fireball, sending it shooting towards him.

It struck him on the shoulder, sending him hurtling backwards into the wall, clothes on fire. He screamed, rolling across the floor to try and dampen the flames. There was a muffled gunshot then he lay still. It looked like he'd shot himself. The conveyor belt stopped.

With a demonic wail, Imelda flew to crouch beside him, sobbing as she rolled him over only to have blood spattered over her uniform. I saw my chance to get her, too, and closed in. But I had to quickly dive for cover as she unleashed a red-hot fireball at me.

'I'm warning you, Gallows,' she hissed. 'If anything happens to my Eli, I'll pull you apart bone by bone and feed you to a pack of hungry pick-tooths!'

'Sure talk a good fight, Imelda,' I replied calmly. 'Why don't you give it up then we can both help Eli.'

'After you clap us in handcuffs first – don't think so, kid. Better if I kill you first then help Eli myself. I'm a better mage than you anyway.'

I overheard Eli croak, 'Get the kid, I'm OK.'

Another single-barrelled stone spitter sat near the far wall and, keeping low to the ground, I weaved my way over to it, hoping that like the others, it was loaded. I had no time to check. I swung the gaping mouth of the thunder dragon towards Imelda then lit the fuse. It *was* loaded. There was a deafening explosion as a boulder tore towards Imelda but somehow she managed to dive out of the way and the stone did nothing more than blow a huge hole in the wall. Noticing me reload, Imelda scrabbled through the hole to escape.

Unholstering my six shot, I chased after her. I found myself in a smaller room containing more weapon-making equipment and another conveyor belt, but there was no sign of Imelda. Lined up on the belt were rows of large demijohn bottles – big thick bottles that usually contained wine or spirits. But these had something else in them. I noticed the outside of the glass seemed to glow with a thin magical light. I felt a chill crawl up my neck. Ghostly pale blue-and-white mist swirled inside the bottles. Then to my horror I saw an eye, horns, clawed hands.

Wraiths!

So that was the secret ingredient Uncle Crazy Wolf and I had been racking our brains to try and figure out. They looked like they'd been shrunk? But how? Why? My heart raced. Then that explained why I'd seen the eye of a wraith staring out of a Death Mace. What magic was this – capturing wraiths to put in bottles? They were obviously restrained by some magical force-field as wraiths can slip through walls easily, even cave walls in Deadrock mines.

The boulder must've blown over a table full of Death Maces in various stages of construction and they lay strewn all over the floor. I lifted one to examine it as a floorboard creaked behind me. I spun round only to see Imelda leap towards me swinging an unlit Death Mace. I parried awkwardly, the impact painfully jarring my shoulder muscles.

Sparks flew from the clash of the iron mace heads. I slashed my mace sideways, aiming for her guts, but she easily recoiled backwards.

'Demons might fear to tread here but we got plenty of wraiths,' said Imelda, her new face splitting open in a grimacing smile. 'Always did like a nice bottle o' spirits!'

'You put wraiths in bottles. But why?'

'Powerful things, spirits, all that dark energy. I just had to figure out a way of harnessing it together with a little magic and a lot of gun powder. Only took a slight modification to the Wynchester Demon Shot to make it a demon scoop. I use compression magic to shrink wraiths into fist-sized spheres of pure evil spiritual energy then I wrap them in gunpowder and some nasty metal – genius!'

She lunged at me, swinging the mace for my head again. I spun out of the way, the mace crashing down on a work bench, sending splinters of wood showering into the air.

I thrashed wildly but she brought her mace back up to block me then hacked mechanically, striking blow after blow that turned my arms into jelly.

I felt a wave of despair wash over me. I couldn't do it. Imelda was just too strong. It was like she was toying with me. Then I thought of Jez back in the other room, lying on that conveyor belt, maybe dying. I had to help her.

Waving her mace, Imelda drove me back, pinning me like a frightened bangtail squirrel against a wooden support beam. She swung her mace with even more venom, hoping to finish me off. I ducked and one of the dagger-sharp mace spikes lodged in the wood, buying me a few vital seconds – seconds I didn't plan on wasting. Cursing, she took one hand off the mace shaft and I saw a fireball begin to form in her palm but before it could, I directed a fist into her scar-free but still ugly mug, hearing her nose crack like Titus Knott's whip. I had a desperate fleeting thought that magic wasn't half as satisfying as a good old punch in the face.

Imelda wailed, pulling the mace free with a sudden burst of strength. But she lost her grip and it flew across the room, crashing into one of the glass jars containing a captured wraith and smashing it to smithereens.

The wraith, suddenly free from its glassy prison, began to grow bigger. Its great horned head, clawed hands and feet and fearsome, staring eyes all returned to their original size as it roared, 'Mmmmmmmrrrrrrrrgggula!'

It fixed both dark eyes on Imelda and although she wore a cavalry uniform, the wraith seemed to sense its captor.

'Nooooooooooooo!' she moaned.

The wraith swept towards her, swathing her in pale shimmering light as its great mouth seemingly swallowed her up.

I shoved my fingers in my ears, unable to bear her screams as the evil spirit mercilessly tore her soul from her body. I figured the wraith would probably get indigestion from Imelda's dark twisted soul.

Was I next? I feared as much and my eyes raked the room looking for a Demon Shot rifle. But the wraith circled the room a few times then disappeared through the factory wall, into the night, as Imelda's soulless body flopped to the floor like it had no bones. Still breathing, she would be like the living dead for a few days, a week at the most, then die.

I hurried back through to the other part of the factory. My muscles ached and my ears rang from the noise of the stone spitters and the shooting. Stepping over Eli, I checked to see if he was breathing. He wasn't.

Jez still lay on the conveyor belt and I rushed over. 'Jez, are you OK?'

'What hit me, the Flyer?'

'You fell from the rafters, don't you remember?'

She stared at me blankly then shook her head. 'My ankle hurts.'

I examined it. 'Looks swollen an' I got no magic leaves left. I'll carry you.'

She got up and tried to walk. 'Ouch! Just let me put my arm round you.'

With Jez hobbling, we made our way slowly across the weapon assembly room. My jaw dropped open when I saw the destruction. Most of the soldiers lay injured or dead. Captain Clint was trapped under a fallen beam but alive. Phlum was lying wailing like a baby, hands over his eyes. Blood covered his trouser leg. I rolled it up.

'It's OK,' I reassured him.

'There's blood, lots of blood. I can't look.'

'It's a scratch, Phlum. Where's the High Sheriff?'

He pointed. 'Don't look good.'

I went over and saw the High Sheriff sitting up nursing a wound on his leg.

'Spirits alive, Will,' he moaned. 'I feel like I've been put through the ore grinder back at the gem mine. Where's Eli?'

'Dead.'

'Imelda?'

'Good as. Wraith got her. Listen, don't try to talk. Rest up, Shy an' I will fly to the fort for help.'

★★★

Outside, Shy trotted over. 'Will, you OK? What the heck was goin' on in there – noise was like the western arm collapsing all over again! Take it ya found them?'

'Easy, Shy, I'm fine.' I stroked her nose. 'We found them all right. It was quite a gunfight.'

'Gunfight,' Shy baulked. 'Sounded more like a full-blown battle. At one point a boulder came whistlin' over my head.'

'Eli firing stone spitters,' I explained. 'A lot of soldiers are injured, so we gotta go for help.'

'Is Jez OK?'

'Twisted her ankle real bad but she'll be fine. What about you an' the other horses?'

'Some were a bit spooked by the flying missiles but we're all right.'

'You up for flying by moonlight, Shy? Quicker we get to the fort, the better.'

'Moonlight's good for me – ain't called Moonshine for nothing.'

We took to the sky. As we flew, Moonshine asked, 'What about that scoundrel Imelda?'

'Dead.'

'Dead – what happened?'

Recalling her expression just before the wraith swallowed her up, I replied, 'She had one bottle of spirits too many.'

CHAPTER FOURTEEN

★

Passing Out

Moonshine's brass bridal rosettes gleamed in the sunlight as we made our way, in procession with all the other trainee's horses, towards the parade ground.

Crowds of folk lined the square and it didn't take long for me to pick out Grandma and Uncle Crazy Wolf, dressed in their smart city clothes, beaming in the front row. I'd heard Grandma was front in line at the fort gate when they'd let the folk in earlier.

I gave Moonshine a pat on the neck. 'You OK, Shy?'

'Legs are wobblier than the wheels of an old cart, but I'm good.'

'You'll be fine. Remember we can't critter chitter much once we're out there in case folk wonder who I'm talkin' to. You'll remember all the drill moves, won't you?'

'You kidding? I've been doing them in my sleep.'

'Can't believe we're finally gonna pass out, Shy. For a while back in Eli's gun factory, I wondered if I'd ever make it out alive.'

'I always knew you would. Take more than that smelly good-for-nothin' wolfer to get the better of a sky cavalry soldier.'

It suddenly hit me that that's exactly what I would be in less than an hour – a fully-fledged sky cavalry soldier. There'd been so much going on of late I hadn't really had a moment to think about today and truly take in what it all meant. I felt different. Sort of older or something. I'd fought Imelda till she was as good as dead. I wasn't proud of that but then we'd lost men too. I guess that's what being a soldier was all about and I was ready to be one.

Imelda's soulless body had been locked up in Mid-Rock City jail to stare at the iron bars of her cell – the real Imelda had been sucked up by a very angry wraith. It didn't look good for her – she'd probably be dead in a few days. It was sad, as she had all that skill to make stuff, yet she had never put it to good use. The stone spitter was an amazing weapon when you considered the intricate carving of the beautiful thunder dragons. The Death Mace, too, had the spark of genius.

The gold had been recovered from the factory along with the magic books Eli pretended Imelda had stolen. With Eli dead, the Wynchester Demon Shot factory was now under the more stable ownership of the High Sheriff until a suitable buyer could be found to take over the running of it – hopefully the new owner wouldn't be a rotten crook like Eli. In the meantime, Uncle Crazy Wolf had offered his services – with the help of the magic books – in working out the spells and processes needed for future production of the Demon Shot.

On a happier note, the slave kids were reunited with their families in Heng-Choke Village and with Titus behind bars, that was the end of slavery in the gem mine and hopefully the rock bottom. The High Sheriff planned a whole new series of tough measures for anyone who thought they could flout the new anti-slavery laws.

The crowd cheered as we entered the parade ground, all of us attired in neat uniforms and caps with a crossed-sabre emblem and carrying rifles and sabres that flashed in the sunlight. The horses, too, were saddled in full military tack including ceremonial sheepskin nose bands. As we marched past the crowds of parents and grandparents, I glanced at Grandma and Uncle Crazy Wolf who gave me a wave. I felt very proud.

The drill sergeant bellowed, 'Draw your sabres! Present arms!'

Responding, I held my sabre in a vertical position, the hilt level with my chin.

A demonstration of military drills followed as we showed off the skills we had learned over the weeks. It was going really well. Like Shy said, we'd practised so many times that it all just came naturally. But then one of the horses did a big smelly dump of manure right in the middle of the parade ground. It lay steaming in front of where Moonshine and I were heading.

Moonshine snorted, a look of disgust on her face. 'Yeeaggh! Did you see that? Now that is just wrong, I mean there's a time and a place...'

I grinned. 'Reckon the excitement gotta bit too much for him.' But I was worried, too, as the manure was directly in our path and it was getting closer.

'Talk about a dung mountain! Stinks, too. We gotta turn back, Will.'

'I can't turn back, Shy. I gotta keep in drill formation.'

Luckily the drill sergeant gave order to halt just as Moonshine was about to walk into it. I breathed a sigh of relief.

The parade ended with the drill sergeant yelling, 'Sky cavalry soldiers ... to your duties.'

I was especially proud as this was the first time we'd all been referred to as a sky cavalry soldiers during the drill.

After the parade I gave Moonshine a pat on the neck. 'You did it, Shy. You're a fully-fledged sky cavalry horse just like your pa – he sure would've been proud of ya today.'

Moonshine rolled a watery brown eye at me.

'Thanks, Will but *we* did it – we're a team and a good one, too. If you hadn't wanted to join the sky cavalry, I wouldn't been standing inside this fort today.'

Jez almost pounced on me with a hug, a beaming smile on her face. Then she saluted me. 'Congratulations, Private Gallows, welcome to the sky cavalry.'

'Thanks, Jez. I couldn't have done it without you. Firstly for putting the idea in my head when you joined up last year, then for mentoring and keeping me right during training.'

'It weren't difficult, Will. You're a natural-born soldier.'

Grandma and Uncle Crazy Wolf were next to appear from the crowd of folk.

Yenene smiled. 'I'm proud of you, Will. You looked good up there.'

'Thanks, Grandma. Sure means a lot you saying that. I hope you understand that this way I get to serve the whole of the rock and not just the elf folk.'

'I'm glad you finally figured out what you wanna do. I reckon ya made a good choice though can't say I won't miss you around Phoenix Rise.'

Crazy Wolf nodded wisely. 'It is good, Will, that you found your own way. Though I hope we haven't lost Roaring Dragon for good.'

'No way, Uncle Crazy Wolf, Roaring Dragon is here to stay, especially with the High Sheriff being OK with me practising elf magic. And I'll still be visiting you in Gung-Choux Village from time to time when I get leave.'

'I went to see Imelda in prison,' he said solemnly. 'It troubled my spirit greatly to see her that way, just staring – soulless. Made harder by the fact her face is now healed. Although older, she has not changed that much from when she was apprenticed under me all those years ago. I couldn't help thinking what a tragedy it is.'

'I think so, too – she had a lot to offer if she hadn't started dabbling in dark magic. What made her do it?'

Crazy Wolf sighed. 'When I was young my grandfather told me a story of a young elf brave who had two wolves inside him, fighting each other. The first was the wolf of peace, love and kindness. The other wolf was fear, greed and hatred. "Which wolf will win, grandfather?" I asked him eagerly. "Whichever wolf the young brave feeds," he replied. So it is with Imelda – she fed the wrong wolf.'

'Overfed it,' I added.

Just then, Phlum appeared, a big grin on his lumpy face. He stuck out a shovel hand and we shook. 'You done great, Will. Congratulations.'

'Thanks, Phlum.'

'Don't forget to look me up if you need some Cure All or if ya wanna go bat riding.' He laughed.

Moonshine, who was standing nearby, must have overheard and gave a whinny of disapproval. I don't think she liked the idea of me riding anything but her.

'Ya found a new place to live yet?' I asked.

'Kinda like it round here, so I been thinkin' I might move up to the Midrock, especially as I'm gonna be helping the High Sheriff. He's asked me to work with him on trying to prevent further damage to the roots by mining.'

'That's good. Hopefully see you around, then.'

I said goodbye to Grandma and Uncle Crazy Wolf. The railway track near Edgewater still hadn't been fixed so they planned to fly home to the eastern arm. Then, I headed for the mess hall. There was a mighty tasty smell wafting from the kitchen. I hadn't touched my breakfast for nerves about the parade so I was hungrier than a scrawny underbear.

★ ★ ★

Later, I climbed the lookout tower for my guard duty. To my surprise, Jez was already up there, rifle by her side.

'Didn't they tell you, I said I'd cover for you? You're bound to be tired after the parade – I couldn't believe they didn't give all the new soldiers a break from duties. No rest for the wicked, huh?'

'Thanks, Jez, but I ain't tired.'

'Well then, I'll keep you company for a bit.'

We stared out over Mid-Rock City, bathed under a ghostly pale full moon, and looked at the crowded

noisy streets on the edge of the city. Pianos tinkled from busy saloons as the troll quarter sprang to life for another night's drinking, brawling and dancing.

'What ya thinkin' 'bout?' Jez asked after a while.

'Imelda.'

'Imelda!' she gasped. 'Reckon she's the last person I'd wanna think about on my passin' out day – if she'd had her way, you wouldn't have been passin' out.'

'Been a lot of talk about slavery and it got me thinking that Imelda was kind of a slave herself.'

'How d'ya mean?'

'She was a slave to dark magic. It was coursing through her veins like frog poison. Every bone in her body was crooked as a barrel full o' gutfish hooks. Hunting and killing pick-tooths and thunder dragons, even being attracted to Eli 'cos he was a crook, too.'

'Your tone of voice sounds like you feel sorry for her.'

'I do a bit. I mean, on one hand I'm glad she ain't around anymore to cause trouble but I'm kinda sad 'cos I reckon she weren't *all* bad. If only she'd fed her good wolf more,' I said, recalling Uncle Crazy Wolf's story.

Jez frowned. 'Fed her good wolf?'

'It's an old elf story Uncle Crazy Wolf was telling me about. There's a good wolf and a bad wolf fighting inside of us – if you feed your good wolf, then it'll win.'

Jez eyes widened. 'Wait, I know that story, 'cept in the dwarf version the evil hungry wolf wins the fight then *eats* the well-fed good wolf.'

I made a screwed up face. 'Ain't it too weak to fight?'

Jez shrugged. 'Maybe hunger drives it to fight better.'

I shivered as in the distance I heard a real pick-tooth howl at the full moon.

Suddenly, bearing her teeth, Jez snapped at me. I quickly drew back. Then we both burst out laughing like a couple of rock hyenas.

THE END

With grateful acknowledgement to
Carolyn Whitaker, London Independent Books,
and Charlie Sheppard and Chloe Sackur,
Andersen Press.

ABOUT THE AUTHOR

As a child **Derek Keilty** would write stories about his stuffed panda, making them into books, folding the pages and drawing the cover. 'I'm still writing stories,' Derek says, 'though now the great folk at Andersen Press do the "making into books" bit which I'm very happy about.'

Probably due to the disappointing experience of never having an author visit his primary school (which he would have loved), Derek makes a point of regularly visiting schools all over Ireland, storytelling and taking story-writing workshops and counts it as one of the 'bestest' things about being a children's author.

Derek lives in Belfast with his wife, Elaine, who is Canadian, and twin daughters, Sarah-Jane and Rebekah, not forgetting Lady, the golden retriever who will do anything for a digestive biscuit. As well as writing, his other hobbies include drawing cartoons, reading and trying to get better at playing guitar.

ABOUT THE ILLUSTRATOR

Jonny Duddle lives in North Wales with his wife and young family. When he is not exploring forests and scrumping apples, he is found sprawled across his studio floor, drawing and busily inventing worlds.

With his background in the computer games industry, Jonny is skilled at character development; he initially works with pencil sketches and then draws and paints straight onto his computer using a Wacom tablet.

Having worked on a pirate ship (climbing up and down riggings), and as an art teacher in the middle of the Kalahari Desert, it is no wonder that his work is so varied. Jonny's first picture book was *The Pirate Cruncher*, and he went on to write several more, including *The Pirates Next Door*, which won the Waterstones Children's Book Prize. Jonny has also illustrated other much-loved books – from Terry Pratchett's *Nation* to the covers for J.K. Rowling's Harry Potter series.

WILL GALLOWS

& THE SNAKE-BELLIED TROLL

DEREK KEILTY

ILLUSTRATED BY JONNY DUDDLE

It's time for revenge!

Will Gallows, a young elfling sky cowboy, is riding out on a dangerous quest. His mission? To bring Noose Wormworx, the evil snake-bellied troll, to justice. Noose is wanted for the murder of Will's pa, and Will won't stop until he's got revenge!

'Wow, what a brilliant read. Fresh and original – and very funny too. This cowboy's riding to an exciting new frontier in fiction.'
Joseph Delaney, author of *The Spook's Apprentice*

9781849392365 £6.99

WILL GALLOWS
&THE THUNDER DRAGON'S ROAR

DEREK KEILTY
ILLUSTRATED BY JONNY DUDDLE

It's time to choose sides!

Sky cowboy Will Gallows is caught up in a bitter land
feud between the cowboy settlers of the eastern arm
and the elf 'braves' of Gung-Choux village.

With battle looming, Will sets out on a quest that leads
him to the rock's edge, where deadly thunder dragons
roam, and where he stumbles
on a treacherous plot to drive
the elf tribes off the eastern
arm forever.

'Action packed, this is an
inventive story with a host of
larger-than-life characters.'
Julia Eccleshare

9781849393287 £6.99

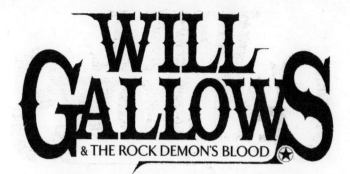

WILL GALLOWS
& THE ROCK DEMON'S BLOOD

DEREK KEILTY
ILLUSTRATED BY JONNY DUDDLE

It's time to face an old enemy!

Will Gallows, a brave elfling sky cowboy, is finding life tough on the ranch. Should he follow his heart and join the elf side of his family, learning all he can of their magical secrets? Or should he report for duty with the sky cavalry?

Will's decision is put on hold when his grandma is kidnapped – by an evil troll like none Will has ever seen before. A troll with extraordinary powers and a long-held grudge to avenge…

'Extremely funny and utterly bonkers' *The Times*

9781849395359 £5.99